Beyond the Headlights

Beyond the Headlights

Allan Davis

IGUANA

Publisher: Meghan Behse
Editor: Paula Chiacros
Front cover design: Ruth Dwight, designplayground.ca
Cover image (wheat field): rajeev ramdas

ISBN 978-1-77180-580-3 (paperback)
ISBN 978-1-77180-579-7 (epub)

This is an original print edition of *Beyond the Headlights*.

Beyond the Headlights is the third novel in the Discards Series. In each book, an early twenties main character finds her way out of a dysfunctional situation: abuse, abandonment, addiction, isolation. The list will never end, so neither will this series.

Other books in the Discards Series

Discards

From Muddy Water

To Chris. I'll see you on the other side.

INTRODUCTION

Like a high-tech radio picks up sound waves across space, a highly intuitive person can pick up the thoughts and feelings of other consciousnesses across space. Carl Jung called this synchronicity.

Jung went one step further. When a person dies, consciousness continues to exist as part of the universal electromagnetic field. Jung suggested the possibility of the transmigration and intersection of consciousnesses of highly intuitive people across both time and space. Jung called this acausal parallelism…

Acausal parallelism is only a theory. There is no scientific proof. But theories shift from improbable to possible to probable to fact all the time. It's not that long ago that the world was believed to be flat.

CHAPTER ONE

Father Clark
May 2009

I was waiting at the front door of the church, which was set back far enough from the gravel road leading to the Broken Deer Double-Wides Trailer Park that I didn't get too much summer dust. I could hear from the basement Aiyana at the piano running her fingers along the keys, up and down, playing "Chopsticks."

When Mr. Skibo arrived, I said, "Don't worry about your shoes. You're here to tune this old Samick piano. And then to hear this little girl play it."

Mr. Skibo opened his leather case. He took out a leaver and wrench and hammer. I watched him plunk and listen and plunk. When he had finished he tidied away his tools. He turned on his tape recorder. "What would you like to play, Aiyana?"

"She can't answer that question," I said. "She simply plays what comes to her from the other side."

"Other side, Father? What other side?"

"She can't explain that. She believes she's two people. First the music comes to her as though she's another person playing on the other side. And then she walks over here to the church to play the music she just heard."

"Acausal parallelism. I've heard of that. But never have I met someone with that gift."

I knew Aiyana was ready, no need for a warm-up. She closed her eyes and I closed my eyes. This was how we did it. For her and for me there was no piano. From the dark, her fingers began to pluck the notes that would play the Chopin that she had just heard on the other side.

I stood back, waiting for the tiny flame that lit this child's heart to burst into this day's miracle of notes: an array of complicated tasks accomplished all at the same time by the dance of those long fingers of those little hands — the right doing one job, the left another; the ten fingers doing ten other jobs; sharps and flats in black and white controlled by timing the rests and trills; one hand in three beats to a measure, and in the other hand, four; the mind reading, interpreting, and locating each chord while the fingers softened here and hardened there. And all this performed by this seven-year-old child, eyes closed in a Zen trance.

When she finished, Mr. Skibo said, "This little girl is astonishing, Father. Never had a lesson, you say? She could be playing on two pianos for the Toronto Symphony."

"Two pianos. That is what is so peculiar. She says she is already playing two pianos."

"I'm sure she feels like she's playing two pianos. Who knows? She's a child and will describe it the best way she can. But whatever it is that allows her to play the way she plays, we can't figure that out here." Mr. Skibo held up the tape. "Something must be done for this child, and I intend to make it happen."

I thanked Mr. Skibo and we shook hands. I stood on the front step of the church as Mr. Skibo got into his car and drove away. A well-intentioned man, but unfamiliar with life in the Broken Deer Double-Wides Trailer Park. Still, he might do something, and something had to start somewhere.

Aiyana went home to help her mother with the laundry, so I sat on the front step of my church. Sitting was something I did often because my new heart meds made me dizzy. I leaned back against the front door and closed my eyes. I wondered what Mr. Skibo thought of these fifty-three double-wides sitting in the middle of this one-square-mile field at the edge of Broken Deer Lake. The man who flew the bush plane said that from the sky the trailer park looked like a hodgepodge of different-coloured boxes in a square of dirty brown stuck on a green wall. He said the lakes are all called Deer because looking down from a bush plane, they're all shaped like deer.

I imagined myself seated next to Mr. Skibo, driving along the gravel road to Highway 69. Let me tell you about life in Broken Deer Double-Wides, Mr. Skibo. Let me explain not what it looks like from a bush plane but what it looks like from my front door. Listen to how it is. In the summer, the younger Broken Deer girls play hopscotch with their cousins on the park office parking lot. The older ones play hide-and-seek in the ice huts. The younger boys go fishing for suckers and shiners. The boys throw the fish up on the bank where they flop in the grass and die and rot in the sun while the boys go home for lunch: canned pork and beans and fried baloney. They call it "Double-Wides Deluxe." After lunch, they go garbage wading at the dump while the bigger boys hang around. They kick things. They spit. They get into fights. They break the windows of the boarded-up houses half a mile along from the trailer park. They play hide-and-seek with the girls in the boarded-up school.

Let me explain what happens to the girls, Mr. Skibo. Winter comes. The younger ones play with the dolls shipped up to this church every Christmas. Every Christmas is white and the white stays until it melts into yellow slush, which turns the trailer park into the dirty brown the bush pilot was talking about, the same colour as the rutted road you were ten minutes ago driving on, dirty brown like the dolls after a long, boring winter.

Springs come and go. The dolls get lost and the girls get older. I tell the parents they shouldn't drink so much and should spend time with their kids and pay more attention to what the older girls are doing with the boys in the ice huts pulled up on shore for the summer.

They're in there fishing, all right. The girls have the bait and the boys have the poles but what they're going to catch won't come out looking like a fish but will come out looking like an unwanted doll.

See me now, Mr. Skibo. I wipe at a tear with the back of my hand. I struggle to my feet. What I mean to say, Mr. Skibo, I look at Aiyana's future and it breaks my heart.

I returned to my apartment at the back of the church and stretched out on my chesterfield. My new meds were making my mind do a lot of drifting. Not that it had anything else to do, mind you. Years ago, yes. But the only thing left at the Sisters of Mercy Church now was the Saturday morning food bank.

Apart from that, Mr. Skibo, have I changed anything here in Broken Deer? Have I accomplished anything? The parents pretend they don't know what goes on in those ice huts. They act like the FAS kids I used to visit at the assessment centre in Sudbury. But the parents aren't FAS. They're drunk, almost the same thing, I guess. Besides, Mr. Skibo, if you add it up, more babies mean more welfare.

Ah well, Mr. Skibo. By now you will have reached the crossroads. You'll be idling at the stop sign. The road sign that used to be there pointing Sudbury this way and Toronto that way got shot so full of holes it's hard to read. There was no point in replacing the sign — it would just get shot full of holes again. That's why right now you're sitting there wondering which direction to choose.

They say, Mr. Skibo, the job of the angels is to give us signs to help us make good choices in life's directions. I have a reproduction of the fifteenth-century painting of the Angel of Mercy, her white wings spread wide, providing protection for a small child huddled at a crossroad. This is the real Angel of Mercy, not the modern Angel of Mercy who brings death.

So, Mr. Skibo, if you've been sent here by the real Angel of Mercy, as I know you have, I pray that, when you make your decision and signal your turn, your direction will return you to Broken Deer to help this little girl called Aiyana.

CHAPTER TWO

Aiyana

I slipped out of bed and, careful not to rattle the rickety aluminum screen, stepped onto the porch of our double-wide trailer. I followed the gravel road through the trailer park to the wooden docks of Broken Deer Lake. The morning sun was bouncing off the whitecaps far out. The waves were tinkling the tin minnow buckets against the outboards tied end to end. Uncle Jimmy's flat-bottom skiff was pulled up, nose-tied to a birch tree, its oars folded back, resting. Most afternoons, Uncle Jimmy would climb into his skiff to sleep off his drinking. He'd lie back in the sunshine with his arms straight out as though he was waiting for someone to row him somewhere.

I found the stray kitten, Socks, licking the open necks of empty beer bottles in the ice-fishing hut next to the skiff. "Don't drink that," I whispered. "It'll make you talk funny and shout and fight and smash up your snowmobile."

I fed Socks yesterday's baloney sandwich that I'd hidden under my pillow. "Made from fresh-caught baloney on sale at Harry's," my mother said. It didn't smell too fresh-caught when I woke up in the middle of the night.

I picked up the kitten. I sat in the grass behind the ice hut and stroked the soft fur. In the sun shining on the kitten's foot, I could see the yellow and the orange and the red that came together to make the colour brown. I cradled the kitten against my cheek and pretty soon the little motor started.

One paw was white, the others brown, like different socks. One of my socks was one shade of blue, the other was a different shade of blue, like the feet of two different children. Most of the other kids in the trailer park got their clothes free from cardboard boxes sent to the Sisters of Mercy Catholic Church from the South, wherever that was, maybe on the other side where the music came from. I don't go there except when I hear the music, because if my mother found out, she'd keep it locked because it'd be too expensive to heat in the winter and too much bother to clean in the summer. But sometimes, when I woke up at night, I thought I could hear my dad on the other side, calling me to come and play the piano. Sometimes I could hear the grinding of the ice I found him in on the shoreline after he fell into the fishing hole at Grandpa Willie's.

Uncle Jimmy said, "What you're hearing is the mice living in the wall between the two halves. Rats in there too. When they tear these trailers apart they find all kinds of things living between the walls. I knew a guy once who lived in a double-wide. He'd wake up hearing boots walking around, on the other side it sounded like. But if he'd go from this side, which was like this trailer with the kitchen and the living room, and then through the door into the other side, which was like here with the bedrooms, he'd hear the boots walking around from the side he'd just come from. So he busted a hole in the wall and found his dead grampa living in there."

Yesterday my mother ate her breakfast of bread and strawberry jam with a beer chaser. "God help me, Jesus, Joseph, and Mary. Down the hatch. Who gives a fuck. It gets me started." That's what she said, like morning prayers. The bread came from Harry's Groceries and Bait. The strawberry jam came from the Sisters of Mercy Food Bank.

Yesterday after breakfast my mother put our dirty clothes into the new washing machine. After last year's flood, every double-wide trailer in Broken Deer got a government-supplied washer and dryer. But since nobody's trailer was wired for dryers, my mother used hers for a TV stand. Millie George's mother used hers to keep boxes of cereal in. "Safe from the mice," she said.

Yesterday, I sat on the front porch and watched my mother hang the clothes on the line. Then it rained and the clothes got wet. Then the sun came out and they got dry. Then it rained and they got wet again. This was why today I was wearing socks that didn't match, as though I was two different people, the same as yesterday.

Each morning, each TV in each double-wide was turned on by a remote, rain or shine, to the same round of programs, one after the other, every day the same. I knew about *same*. Same cars and same boats that stayed the same colour in the same spot in front of the same double-wides day after day, month after month, always the same. Same seemed round too, like a plate, like a satellite dish, like a toilet.

During yesterday's rain, while my mother and Uncle Jimmy worked through their two-four of Moosehead under the porch awning, I watched a Doctor Roberts rerun on our satellite flatscreen. When I heard voices outside, I got up and looked out the front window. The Ranger Rescue, two men in a white Ford Ranger called the Drunk Truck, pulled up in front of our double-wide. Because it had been raining for two days, instead of going down to the docks to sleep it off in his skiff, Uncle Jimmy had passed out on our porch. The men got on either side of him and took him down the porch steps and laid him flat on his back snoring in the box of the pickup. He got locked up somewhere to dry out so he wouldn't cause trouble.

But today he was back, sitting with my mother on the porch, picking at the scabs on his face, drinking a hair-of-the-dog from a two-four of Moosehead, almost drunk again. *Again* was a word like *same*. It was raining again, the same as yesterday. I was watching a Doctor Roberts rerun again, the same as yesterday.

Dr. Roberts lived in a real house with an upstairs and a downstairs and a front lawn with a flower garden. This episode was about Sunday dinner. Mrs. Roberts set the table, each plate between the fork on one side and the knife on the other. Each plate looked round, the same as the word *again* seemed round. It was like the laundry, dry and wet and dry again. It was like my mother, drunk and sober and drunk again. It was like going round and round in circles, like water in the toilet bowl after it's flushed. But not when the septic was flooded. Then the water spilled out on the floor.

Dr. Roberts sat at one end of the table and Mrs. Roberts at the other end. The children, Sally and Johnny, seven and nine, sat at either side. Today was Johnny's turn to say grace. "For what we are about to eat."

That one.

The program ended with Dr. Roberts reading a bedtime story to the two children propped up on pillows in Sally's bedroom. No strange noises came from between her walls, which were covered with pictures of kittens, some with different-coloured socks. I turned off the TV with the remote. I cradled Socks in my arms and round and round we went, spinning in rerun circles across the living room, into the kitchen, onto the porch.

"Yer gonna make yerself dizzy," said Uncle Jimmy.

My mother snapped open another Moosehead and lit another cigarette.

Uncle Jimmy wasn't my real uncle. His name was Jimmy George and his daughter was Millie George and she was in grade three where I should have been but wasn't because I had trouble learning.

"Aiyana, give that cat to Uncle Jimmy. He needs a cat at his house to catch mice." As though my mother couldn't remember saying it, she said, "Uncle Jimmy'll take that cat home to his house. For the mice."

The rain was coming down harder. I knew I could hide Socks at the church, but by the time I got there, Socks would be soaking wet and would catch a cold. But that would be better than living with Jimmy George. I stood close to the top step, my back against the wall, ready to run if Uncle Jimmy decided to take my kitten.

I waited. In two kitchen chairs, my mother and Jimmy sat tipped back against the aluminum siding. Usually about now, Uncle Jimmy would start telling stories about working at the Historic Trails Motel and Restaurant. He got paid in pints of beer plus a room with a hot plate so they didn't take away his welfare cheque. But he got fired after he smashed up his snowmobile that he shouldn't have been driving because it was summer and he was drunk. And because the man who owned Historic Trails owned the ice hut Uncle Jimmy had smashed into.

Uncle Jimmy finished his Moosehead and started on another. He said, "My cousin worked at Historic Trails before me. He was dumb-witted. He couldn't read or write, same as Aiyana, but he knew all about haunted houses and gave people messages from dead relatives and uncles, like Aiyana. Now he's the dishwasher so he gets free leftovers."

My mother finished her Moosehead and started another. "Aiyana won't eat nothing but baloney 'cause it's round. She'll eat green peas 'cause they're round. She won't eat corn 'cause she don't like the colour. And mushrooms she don't like 'cause they got no colour. I went and bought a bunch of purple grapes and a bunch of green grapes — remember that day they somehow got grapes up here to Harry's Grocery? — and I said—"

"Dead kids too," said Uncle Jimmy. "My cousin was good with dead kids. Some people are good with kids."

"Some man came by yesterday," said my mother. "He had a funny name — Skibo."

"That's Russian."

"He was tunin' the church piana and he heard Aiyana play and he wondered if I could get her into a gifted music program. He talked kinda fancy. He called me Mrs. Waters. I said, 'Look aroun'. Does it look like there's a lot of gifted music programs around here?' He says, 'Aiyana should have a conservertary teacher and be working on two pianas.' I says, 'Look aroun'. Does it look like there's a lot of extra pianas aroun' here? I can't afford to feed her never mind pay for conservertary piana teachers with two pianas.'"

"I seen once on television," said Jimmy George, hoisting one cowboy boot against the porch railing, "about a man who couldn't sing or whistle or hold a tune worth a shit."

My mother opened her purse for her cigarettes. "Aiyana can hold a tune, all right. Her brains is full of tunes like her brains is full of colours. But if she looks at a page of writing, she says it looks like spiders."

"Spiders, yeah. He got struck by lightning and saw spiders climbing up his pant leg, made him skip and dance across the floor fer about ten minutes. After that, he could play any instrument they gave him."

My mother looked through her purse for her lighter. "I sure as hell can't afford to feed no stray cats. Give it to Uncle Jimmy, Aiyana, and he'll give it a housekeeping job at his house catching mice."

Uncle Jimmy didn't have a house. He didn't have a double-wide. He didn't have a single wide. He didn't even have a room anymore. Uncle Jimmy tipped back his Moosehead and finished it off in one gulp. He said into his burp, "I knew a man once got shot deer hunting. Had a piece of the bullet stuck in his brain they couldn't take out. Every time he leaned over, he heard his dead wife callin' him fer supper."

My mother lit her cigarette and sucked it in. In her mouthful of smoke the words curled into grey ghosts as she said, "I says to the piana man, 'How's she gonna figure out them notes if they look like spiders?'"

"I heard about a guy once—"

"Skibo his name was."

"That's Russian."

I saw the rain had slowed to a drizzle.

"I knew a Russian guy once who had the power to turn off streetlights. He'd be walkin' along the street and the light would go off. If he concentrated on doin' it, it wouldn't work. When it would happen or where, he couldn't predict. That's how psychic stuff works."

"Maybe that's what Aiyana is. She can't learn at school but she can play the piana better than Elton John."

"Two queers walked into a bar, and the one queer says to the…"

I stepped off the porch. The rain had stopped. Socks cuddled in my arms, I waded through the wet knee-high grass to the bare dirt path running beside the gravel road that ran from the lake through the rows of aluminum double-wides to the gate onto Highway 69. Each double-wide had beside it a car that didn't run or a boat that wouldn't float. But at the top of each roof, perched there like a plastic decoration from last year's dead Christmas tree, was a satellite dish, the same shape and colour as a toilet bowl.

Sometimes our toilet didn't work right, because the rain in the pipes of the double-wide got mixed up with the water in the pipes of the septic. Sometimes my brain didn't work right, because the words of the live people on this side got mixed up with the words of the dead people on the other side. But for some reason the satellites on the roofs always worked right. They brought signals from a tower someplace near the fire lookout and across the top of the sky where you couldn't see them and down through the roofs and into the TVs of each of the fifty-three double-wides waiting there until someone sat down to watch them. For some reason the satellite in my head always worked right. It brought the notes of the music down from the other side and into my brain and into each of my ten fingers waiting there until I sat down to play them.

Sometimes Father Clark said my head was like a double-wide, my brain on this side, my satellite system on the other side. Sometimes he said I was like an electric conductor picking up stuff the rest of us couldn't hear or see. But I said, "I don't know what it is, Father. But I know what it feels like, that the world outside of me is a giant stew and because I'm like two people I got two spoons."

I arrived at the Sisters of Mercy Catholic Church. Father Clark's car stood in the gravel driveway. His dog, Farley, was standing inside the apartment door, waiting to go out, which he did when I stepped in. I found Father Clark in the church basement. He said, "Come on in, Aiyana. Don't worry about wet shoes. I'll mop the floor. The exercise will do me good."

I sat in my usual chair at the chrome-legged kitchen table. "Is it wrong to want to adopt a stray kitten, Father?"

"No, it isn't, Aiyana."

"Why isn't it?"

"The same reason I adopted Farley. Because he needed my help. Because he came to me and asked to be looked after. Because he was hungry. Because when winter comes he'll freeze in the snow. Because he needed to be loved."

Father Clark stroked along Socks's head and scratched behind one ear. "I think this little adoptee wants some milk."

He took the container from the refrigerator and poured some into a dish. Socks knelt and curled her white tail around her hind legs, setting its white tip down beside the white sock as she lapped at the white milk, careful not to get any on her nose or on her whiskers or on the floor, not like Farley, who slobbered and knocked over his dish and spilled everything.

Father Clark checked his clock hanging on the wall next to his picture of John the Baptist standing in the Broken Deer River with Jesus. "It's five minutes before three o'clock, Aiyana. Time for a glass of ginger ale."

Every afternoon we did the same thing at the same time, each with a tall glass with one stir stick and one ice cube fizzing in silvery bubbles and one slice of yellow lemon floating on the top.

"Tell me how the weekend went, Aiyana. I saw you with some other kids at the docks." He set my glass in front of me.

"They hid my shoes so everyone could see my socks."

Father Clark looked. "They don't match. So what?"

"They chased me into the ravine and made Bucky Beaver kiss me. They locked me in the ice hut full of drowned bodies."

"Drowned bodies?"

"They think I can talk to drowned people."

Father Clark looked away before the next question. "Who locks you up?"

"Sarah and Denny and Names. They—"

"Names?"

"They call him Names because he's got three: Timothy Andrew John…"

"They don't know any better, Aiyana."

"It's the teasing, Father."

"Words, Aiyana, sometimes full of meaning, sometimes no more than empty bubbles in the ginger ale. Nothing but fizzle. Like the ice cube, cold for a few minutes and then melted and gone. Like the slice of lemon, sour at first. But" — he used the stir stick to fish the lemon from the glass — "now I'll taste it, to make sure it's turned from sour to sweet." He tasted the lemon. "And now what's left, Aiyana, is the ginger ale, which by drinking will take away the fizzle and the sour of life, and you'll feel better."

"But not like drinking Moosehead."

"Definitely not like drinking Moosehead."

I sat and watched the silvery fizzle turn from bubbles to nothing. I watched the ice melt away and be gone. I put the lemon into my mouth and sucked away the juice, which had turned from sour to sweet. Then I drank the ginger ale and I felt better.

I rinsed both glasses in the sink. I carried Socks to the front of the church basement, pulled up a chair, and seated her in the front row so she could see and listen and maybe someday learn to clap her paws like in an audience. Then I climbed onto the piano stool and began searching among the black-and-white keys for the notes that had come from the other side into my brain the night before. All I had to do was let my fingers find them.

CHAPTER THREE

Father Clark

I stood next to the piano, leaning over to watch the fingers of this little seven-year-old child find the music. She always started with her right hand, testing chords at random, it seemed, before the left hand joined in. Not too far along, I was able to guess where she was going. "I think that's another Chopin. Where did you hear it, Aiyana?"

"It's not really hearing, Father. The music comes to me but not by hearing."

"I think that might be Grande Polonaise."

"I don't know, Father."

Her eyes, as usual, were closed as her hands searched across the keys, organizing into patterns the individual notes of the concerto stored somewhere, somehow, in her mind, waiting to be released by those little fingers as soon as they were ready to begin.

"Why do you do that, Aiyana?" This was only one of the questions I needed someone to explain so I could understand this child's genius.

"Do what, Father?"

"You find the notes. I understand that. Then before you start you…" I wiggled my hand and flexed my fingers. "You stretch the fingers and pull at them. Then you bend each one way back. It looks like they're going to pop right out of the joint."

"They can't play if they're attached to my hands, Father. So I wiggle them loose and break them off. Then I close my eyes and watch my fingers find the notes."

"How do the fingers know which key to land on if your eyes are closed?"

"My fingers follow the fingers that play the piano on the other side."

"But who is on the other side?"

"It's like a shadow, Father, always there but you can't pick it up."

"But where is the music?"

"I close my eyes and the music comes to me like somebody left the radio on."

"And why only Chopin?"

"I don't know, Father."

"And sometimes you go from one Chopin to another."

"When I think I hit a wrong note, I don't stop. I follow it and it takes me to a different piece."

"But you don't see the individual notes, Aiyana? You don't see the piano keys?"

"I see the melody, Father, in coloured patterns."

"See the melody? You mean you don't hear the melody?"

"The notes are like wavy ribbons on different-coloured air."

"I don't understand what you mean by different-coloured air."

"It's easy, Father. The fingers follow the notes and the notes follow the colours, like kite tails follow the kites."

"Where to?"

"I don't know, Father. I have to play now."

I pulled my chair to the front row beside Socks. I was like that piano, the harmony was inside me, but on most days the only one who could find it was this little girl. I leaned back in my chair and, closing my eyes like her, felt the music lift my ailing heart from the drudgery: the Broken Deer families destroyed by unemployment, the town of Broken Deer wrecked by the pulp-and-paper mill shutdown, the Broken Deer church emptied by despair.

When she finished, I wanted to say, Play it again, child. Play it once more for an old priest tired from another day's mopping. Play it one more time for this old heart that has more bad days than good, more notes out of tune than in. Unlike this old piano, each precision note carried by two hundred thirty lengths of steel stretched tight under forty thousand pounds of pressure, each wire struck by a hammer at sixty miles an hour to zing from fifty to ten thousand vibrations per second, and each beat from the fingers of this little girl carried by two hundred thirty miles of veins and arteries to the tired heart of this old priest.

CHAPTER FOUR

Dear Father Clark,

Thank you for bringing this remarkable little girl to my attention. I have listened to the CD. Indeed, a gifted child.

However, after Mr Skibo explained Aiyana's background, I began to have doubts. I wondered, what is a doublewide trailer? So, I looked it up: two identical mirror image parallel structures side by side with a doorway allowing physical passage from one side to the other. Then I wondered, what is a parallel universe? So, I looked it up: Two identical mirror image parallel realities side by side, allowing metaphysical passage from one side to the other. Then I wondered, what is metaphysical passage? So, I looked it up: Passage from the normal to the paranormal; the tangible to the intangible. Then I wondered, how is any of this related to the notion that this little girl has the gift of acausal parallelism?

She doesn't. Acausal parallelism is linked not to music but to intuition. We all have intuition, but some more than others. Carl Jung termed this heightened sense of intuition "synchronicty," the transmigration and intersection across space of the consciousnesses of one person with that of a second. Jung then went one step further and suggested the possibility of the transmigration and intersection across both space and time of the consciousness of a live person to that of a dead person.

So, then I wondered, why does Father Clark think this little girl has the gift of acausal parallelism? The answer is simple. Like most savants, Aiyana can play the music of any concerto she hears. Like all savants, when she seats herself at the physical piano and plays a concerto, she feels like she has been transported into the metaphysical reality of that concerto, in Aiyana's case Chopin. Unlike most savants, Aiyana lives in a physical double wide. A child who lives in a physical doublewide will answer in the voice of a child who, when playing the piano, feels in a metaphysical doublewide.

So, then I wondered, why does this little girl play only Chopin? The answer is simple. She is hearing Chopin's concertos from somewhere, but that somewhere is not "the other side." The most likely explanation is that she is picking up from the background music of some TV program bits and pieces of Chopin. Her disability that prevents her brain from processing linear learning has heightened her brain's ability to process gestaltic learning. While the linear part of her brain is struggling to follow the TV plot line, the gestaltic part of her brain is recording every note, nuance, and chord of the TV background music, in her case Chopin.

That does not mean, Father Clark, that I have not recognized Aiyana's potential. I have referred her to social services here in Toronto. They are going to make a connection with the Sudbury office and get her into a gifted program in her area.

Please keep me informed of Aiyana's progress.

Sincerely,

Dr. Jerry McCoy

Dear Dr. McCoy,

Thank you for your detailed letter.

Although very few of us live in a physical double wide, we all live in a metaphysical doublewide. Although our body lives among the tangibles, our consciousness lives among the intangibles. Every kid taking piano lessons learns to play "Chopsticks." If no pianos existed, and no kids existed, and no sheet music existed, the pattern of notes that come together to create the tangible "Chopsticks" would still exist in the reality called the intangibles. All that would be needed to bring "Chopsticks" back into a tangible reality is for someone to bring back the pattern of notes for "Chopsticks" and play it on a piano. Similarly, every mathematician understands the Theorem of Pythagoras. But if no mathematicians existed, and no tangible triangles existed, the Theorem of Pythagoras would still exist independent of any tangible triangle. In other words, the tangibles on this side are copies of the intangibles on the other side, hence doublewide realities.

The body lives among the tangibles, but consciousness lives among the intangibles. The consciousness that exists in my head called "Me" or "I" exists independent of the chair I am sitting in and the house I am living in. In fact, the consciousness called "me" or "I" exists independent of any tangible reality because it exists only in my head. If my tangible body no longer worked well enough to carry my head around, my consciousness would still exist, providing my brain was still doing its job of keeping the vital parts working.

But when my brain stops working will my consciousness stop existing? If it can exist independent of all tangibles, why would it not continue to exist independent of that tangible called my brain? Brain and body work together to make survival in our tangible reality possible. This is called awareness. A dog has awareness. Awareness is what the brain does. How this works has been extensively studied by neuroscience. But how self-awareness, the "me" and "I" of consciousness works, neuroscience has no clue.

If this consciousness called "me" or "I" is able, like "Chopsticks," to transmigrate between tangible and intangible, then to suggest the possibility of the transmigration and intersection of two independent consciousnesses across time, space, life, and death is not a big stretch.

Here is where intuition enters the discussion. You suggested acausal parallelism was not about music but about intuition. So, I wondered, why does Dr. McCoy think music is not about intuition? Intuition happens when we go from sight to insight, from the five senses to what is called the sixth sense. You say, never having seen or heard this child, that she is picking Chopin up from the TV. But she does not use any of her five senses to play the music. She does not play the music; the music plays her. The music happens.

Seeing is believing. All that I ask is that you let me bring you this child so that you can use your five senses to experience her music "happening."

Sincerely,

Father Clark

CHAPTER FIVE

Father Clark

A few days later I heard a knock on my apartment door. The stranger standing before me was tall and fit, wearing a blue suit with a matching blue tie. I assumed he was a Mountie, come to investigate the recent assault with a deadly weapon, a fight over a woman at the Double-Wides Dance.

His name was Jeffrey, he said. Jeff for short. He didn't talk like a Mountie. His voice was soft and caring. He was a social worker and he wanted to help.

"I have a letter here from Mr. Skibo, Father. He claims one of your little parishioners is an undiscovered genius."

Social workers were not welcome in Broken Deer. But I got into Jeff's car and we drove past Harry's and through the hodgepodge of aluminum-clad trailers sitting askew on cement blocks, past the dogs, boats, cars, kids, snowmobiles, and garbage cans to Mona Waters's front door. Luckily, Aiyana was at the docks, catching shiners for Socks.

We stood under the porch awning. Jeff explained the reason for his visit. "It seems Aiyana has a gift, Mrs. Waters, and with that gift comes a disability. Without further testing, we won't know for certain what her condition is, but here is what we would like to do. Mr. Skibo and I went to the Faculty of Music at the University of Toronto and talked to Dr. McCoy. He explained how the brain of the savant works. It's very complicated. But I read up about it so I could explain it to you. Her phonographic mind allows her to play on the piano anything she hears. The notes are automatically programmed into her brain the same way the words other kids see and hear are automatically programmed into their brains. But here's the problem. Her brain can process spoken words but can't process written words. It's a neurological problem, something to do with the brain pathways. The gift is also a limitation."

Mona looked too hungover to understand anything Jeff was saying, but he persisted.

"Her brain wants to process the written words like it processes the music — a linear, nonlinear problem; language is linear, music is not. The result is some form of dyslexia. Aiyana's brain will probably be seeing fifty different variations of the same printed word, just like her brain hears fifty different variations of the same chord. Sometimes, she'll see words in colour. Sometimes, she'll see them in three dimensions. Sometimes, the words in different colours will jump off the page and move around, like the notes of music. They don't, of course, but that's what it seems like in her mind. That's why she can play the piano but can't read a book.

"Her condition has a scientific name. It's called synesthesia. But Aiyana's brain has an added feature. She plays only Chopin, yet there seems no way that she could ever have heard Chopin. There's no explanation for that other than a very rare phenomenon called acausal parallelism, when two persons unrelated in time and place become connected. In music, it's when two persons unrelated in time and place are able to create identical note- and chord-sequencing patterns, like the one is tuned into the other, a connection that happens through intuitional connections to parallel existences. In plain English, Mrs. Waters, we all have intuition, but some people have heightened awareness intuition. Aiyana has the special edition. That, Mrs. Waters, is why she sometimes feels like she is two people."

Mona blinked. "How's that? You say she really is two people?"

"Well, no, she's not. But that's what it feels like to her. Or look at it this way. We're standing side by side, you and I, barely two feet apart, but you don't feel what I feel. You don't see what I see. You don't do as I do. So it's like we're in two parallel universes. Nevertheless, because we are both in the present, it's possible for our two parallel universes to intersect through intuition. The term often used is chemistry but really this is intuition. We all have it. But Aiyana got the extra special edition that allows her to intersect not only with someone in the present but also with someone in the past and likely with someone in the future."

It should have been early enough in the day for Mona to be sober, but I could smell the alcohol and I was four feet away.

"What good's this special edition gonna do for her if she can't read and write?"

"We'll find the money for her to have special testing, maybe spend a week or so at the university's Faculty of Music, and then go to the next step."

Mona Waters searched through her purse for her cigarettes and lighter. "The music won't do her no good if she can't read and write."

She slipped the purse under one arm and sparked the lighter and leaned the cigarette into the flame.

"After the testing," continued Jeff, "we'll get her help with the reading. But she needs to be in a school with a gifted program. Father Clark was telling me on the way over that he thinks some churches in Sudbury might be able to raise money to help pay, like a sponsorship program."

Aiyana's mother dragged on her cigarette. She put on her familiar I-don't-know-what-you're-talking-about look. I felt my heart, ailing as it was, change from patience with Mona to determination to get Aiyana into Jeff's car where she could look out the back window and watch all the broken people and broken cars and broken boats and broken trailers of Broken Deer blur away and disappear. While Jeff explained, I watched his face change from a good-intentions look to a how-can-I-get-this-little-genius-away-from-this-woman-and-this-place look.

Mona tucked the cigarettes and lighter into her purse. "You mean you want to take her away?" She jetted out the drag of smoke.

I knew what Mona was seeing in that smoke that was costing her seven dollars a pack: herself — looking into the back window of this guy's car, watching her disabled-child allowance blurring away and disappearing from her broken-porch Moosehead afternoons with Jimmy George.

"It's almost summer," she said. "We'll decide when summer's over."

Ah yes. That's how it was done in Broken Deer. Look after the problem some other summer.

Back in the car, I said, "Look around, Jeff. The kids live in these trailers almost on top of one another. There are no green lawns bordered by nice shrubbery. There are no sidewalks to walk on and no flower gardens to not walk on. Look around. In this mishmash of double-wides, there are no fences with square corners and there are no locked gates."

I took a deep breath to let my ticker catch up with my words. "But perhaps you noticed that I have flowers growing across the front of the church behind a white picket fence. Perhaps you noticed the square corners of that fence and the painted hinges of the little gate that opens to let Aiyana in and shuts to keep her tormentors out. She opens the gate and walks into the yard and she shuts the gate and walks into the church and she feels safe."

It was time for my pill, so I was feeling off, but I continued, "Picture what I'm telling you, Jeffrey. I hide a key for Aiyana in a little hidey-hole under the back window. When she wants to play the piano, she reaches in and feels along the brick for the key and when she's finished she puts it back. The church belongs to the community, but the door of the church is locked to the community, and the key is hidden, and only this small child knows where it is."

Another deep breath and I continued, "No one bothers to lock their doors up here, Jeffrey. But I lock the doors of the church so that anyone too drunk to make it home doesn't get sick on the pews. I tell

Aiyana, 'They're called pews. But that's not how I want them to smell.' And she smiles her cute little smile and she nods, understanding the pun. She's not dumb, you see. She's very intelligent. I see it when I look into her eyes. She has amazing eyes that tell me she sees more than the rest of us can see. A well-known fact: Since our world is too complex for our mind to process most of the information it receives, it sorts through just enough basic stuff to allow us to get by without needing to deal with that complex jumble of possibilities that surround us. I think that is what Aiyana means when she says the other side."

Jeffrey pulled up in front of the church. "So where's her father?"

"Drowned last year. He was a good person. He worked in the office at the mill before it closed. As an accountant. That February he drowned. That spring the mill closed. So Mona and Aiyana moved to the trailer park."

"And she has no one else, like an aunt or an older sister?"

"Her grandfather, Willie, is a good man. He works in logging camps in the winter and as a fishing-and-hunting guide in the spring, summer, and fall. He takes Aiyana with him when he can."

Jeffery declined a cup of coffee and set off, promising to do what he could.

...

Next afternoon, returning from the Sudbury library, entering the church basement, I knew something was wrong. Aiyana was there. But she was not playing the piano. She was sitting at the kitchen table. When I glanced around the room I felt my breath catch in my throat. I headed to the washroom so she wouldn't see my tears. I stood at the mirror with my hands on either side of the sink, a short old man with a stout body and an apple-pie face, my white skin getting more pasty pale as the days dragged on. But now my face was not pale and pasty. It was flushed red, not a good sign.

I turned on the cold tap and wiped away the tears with a damp face cloth. I came out of the washroom and considered the mess.

Someone had smashed the piano. The axe lay on the floor beside the stool, also smashed. I took Aiyana's hand and sat her on one of the chrome-legged chairs lined up against the wall.

"The only thing in Broken Deer that has ever been in tune," I said, taking the chair beside her.

"Don't tell my grandfather."

This was Thursday. Her grandfather was coming on Friday to take her on a guide trip. I knew that if Willie learned about the smashed piano, he wouldn't leave the trailer park until he found the piano smasher. He'd go from double-wide to double-wide with the axe until he found who owned it, and then he would explain that axes were used for felling trees, not smashing pianos.

"I'll get you another piano." I heard the rasp in my voice and felt tears in my eyes. I tried to blink them away. I heaved a tired sigh. "They're angry at everything, Aiyana: this church, this place, life, themselves. They don't know what to do with their anger."

"Don't tell my grandfather."

No secrets in Broken Deer. I went with the grandfather to each trailer. Despite his size — I guessed about six foot six — Willie was soft-spoken and polite. He said at each door, "Clarky and I are wondering if you're missing an axe."

We went as far as unit 26 on the lake side of the park. I didn't know the man. I didn't like the look of the trailer, nor did I like the blaring of the TV. Willie's knock was answered by three hundred pounds of unshaven hairy fat barely covered by a grimy undershirt and rumpled shorts.

"That's my axe," he said, his breath smothering me with a mixture of alcohol and tobacco, almost as revolting as he looked. To antagonize this character would be like stepping on a rabid caveman's toe.

The man's expression didn't change as he leaned one shoulder against the doorjamb and listened to Willie explain that Clarky would not press charges but wanted the piano replaced. Without moving away from the doorway, the caveman reached behind to grab a beer that was sitting on the TV. "Her piano playing keeps me awake. I work the night shift. I have to be able to perform according to a standard of productivity or I'll be fired. It's me or the piano."

I was startled by this level of diction from a caveman. Perform according to standards of productivity. His even having a job seemed to be an obvious lie, unless he worked nights as a guard dog in a scrapyard.

Willie looked in the direction of the church. "The piano is away over there. How can you hear that far?"

I stepped in. "She gets pretty loud. It's possible."

Willie said, "I'll buy another piano. But I'm keeping the axe. If you get any more ideas about smashing my piano, I'll be back with your axe."

TEN YEARS LATER

CHAPTER SIX

Aiyana

Millie George and I had gone with one of the gravel workers to a zombie movie at the drive-in near Sudbury. We sat side by side in his pickup, Millie in the middle. Millie put the popcorn between her legs and said, "Help yourself." When the gravel worker did, I left so they could do it in private.

Next time, I went to the drive-in with Catherine Beaver and two gravel guys in a Honda. Catherine was the granddaughter of my mother's aunt. They lived in the double-wide next to Harry's Groceries and Bait. Catherine and I sat in the back seat. While the zombie movie was playing, the two gravel guys sat in the front acting stupid and passing the coke bottle mixed with whisky back and forth. I shook my head, but Catherine didn't.

After the movie, we drove out the bush road past the closed-down sawmill and stopped by the river. The driver said, "Let's switch." So Catherine, already sort of drunk, got into the front, and the other gravel guy, new to the pits, his face pale as a toad's belly, joined me in the back. When he tried to help himself, I got out and walked home.

...

I couldn't remember the exact day my mother's new boyfriend arrived. I could play the piano better than Elton John but had trouble remembering what day it was.

"Today is the fifteenth," Father Clark would say. I'd wonder, What happened to all those other days with all the other numbers?

Hartley worked at the weigh station. Hartley was forty-nine. He was tall and lanky. The horseshoe of hair around his bald head was six inches long. He kept a pistol in the glove compartment of the '69 Caddy he'd just bought from Jimmy George and was going to fix up. He wore the same plaid shirt, work pants, and boots every day. Sometimes he took off the shirt to show me the blue-and-red Ray Price tattoo on his right bicep. He was the best arm wrestler in the pits, and his grip could crush a man's hand. When he was drunk, which he usually was, his joints sagged from his frame like loose hinges.

Hartley and my mother were sitting in the kitchen drinking Moosehead. He said, "Your mother told me you want to learn to drive. I can teach you."

His arm resting on the kitchen table had a Merle Haggard tattoo. I thought, if he were twenty years younger he'd have a ring in one ear and a Megadeth tattoo on his neck. I said, "Only if you haven't been drinking."

We drove the Caddy out the gravel-pit road and stopped at the fire lookout. Hartley wanted to take pictures of me sitting on the front fender. Then he wanted to take some of me standing in front of Smokey the Bear. His leering picture-taking was creepy, but I wanted to learn to drive. I got behind the wheel and touched the gas. The Caddy felt like driving a lumber barge with my grandfather's sixty-horse inboard on the back end.

Afterwards, Hartley dropped me off at Harry's. I bought a big bottle of ginger ale and headed to the church, my sandals crunching in the roadside gravel then slap-slapping when the path turned to dirt. The weigh station's twelve-o'clock whistle screeched as a pickup approached from behind. It slowed down beside me, and the driver stuck his head out the window and asked if I wanted a ride.

"No thanks," I said, without looking at him. "I'm on my way to the church."

"Church is on Sunday."

"It's my job. I'm the church cleaner."

He followed along beside me. "How would you like to do some cleaning for me?"

I walked on, trying to pretend he wasn't there. Then Hartley's Caddy rattled up and parked crossways in front of the pickup, blocking the road. Hartley got out. The other guy got out. He was built like a black bear with a round body and small black eyes. He was twice the size of Hartley.

"Has this gravel-head moron been bothering you, Aiyana?"

"No."

Hartley turned to the man. "Okay. Sorry, buddy. No hard feelings." Hartley extended his hand. "Put 'er in the vice, buddy." The gravel worker took it. But when he tried to pull it free, he couldn't. His little black eyes changed from dull to electrified as Hartley forced him to his knees and his finger bones crunched together.

Hartley left the gravel worker on his knees and got into the Caddy. "Don't forget your lesson tomorrow. I'll meet you at Harry's, same time." He drove away.

The gravel worker got up and drove off one-handed. His pickup disappeared into the road dust, in a hurry to get to Harry's for some Tylenol.

CHAPTER SEVEN

Father Clark

Over the phone, I made arrangements to meet Dr. Jerry McCoy, chair of the Faculty of Music at the University of Toronto. Dr. McCoy explained he was interviewing a new PhD student from Queen's at the Red Brick Coffee Shop in downtown Toronto. Dr. McCoy said, "Why not join us. I'm sure Janine will be interested in your savant. How will we recognize one another? Well, I'm forty-six, tall with greying hair, and probably wearing a tweed sports jacket and jeans."

That seemed to be the big-city style nowadays, a suit jacket with work pants.

"I'm a priest. But I won't be wearing my clerics. I'm short, balding, overweight, and retirement age, which is the reason for the meeting. Before I leave, I have something I must do."

I arrived right on time, 9:00 a.m. It was an unusually warm May day. I took a seat at one of the black tables along the red brick wall near the back. Dr. McCoy and Janine, who looked to be in her early twenties, arrived ten minutes later. Janine was wearing a skimpy tank top and shorts, normal big-city attire for young women nowadays.

We shook hands, Dr. McCoy smiling, Janine's red nails flashing. Right away, I noticed Dr. McCoy's up-down interest in Janine as she took the seat opposite him.

I began. "I'm sure you know why I'm here."

Dr. McCoy nodded. "The little seven-year-old. She could play anything Chopin wrote but never had a lesson and never heard a Chopin piece of music. According to the story, anyway." He glanced at Janine. "But we academics don't believe in stories, not without evidence." He smiled, perhaps hoping she would notice how the corners of his eyes crinkled into crow's feet. Young women liked that apparently. It was something to do with the idea of the father figure and the younger female's biological need of the guarantee of a regular breakfast and dinner.

The waitress arrived to take our order: a coffee for Janine and the same for me.

Dr. McCoy ordered a coffee and scone. "I come here every morning before I go to the university. I'm a bit late today. I was a guest on the CBC's Find the Music with Byron Baird."

"Find the Music," said Janine. "I love that program." She leaned over to shift her large purse from her lap to the floor, revealing a generous bust. Girls showed themselves off like that nowadays. But not Aiyana. She had no interest in a father figure or in a regular breakfast and dinner.

"I've brought a tape recording," I said. "She's almost eighteen now."

Dr. McCoy placed his hands palms down on the table and splayed his fingers. "Skibo took photographs. The one I remember was her hands on the piano keys. 'The hands of a musical genius,' he said."

Janine's smile at Dr. McCoy showed a row of perfect white teeth. "Your area of expertise."

Dr. McCoy shifted in his chair, opened his sports jacket, and arranged himself. "I did studies on the blind woman, Leslie Lemke, who could play Tchaikovsky — never had a piano lesson. That led me to research tone and colour synesthesia."

Janine leaned forward, her blue eyes inquisitive. "I've heard that term before. But I've never understood it."

Dr. McCoy seemed eager to explain. "Musical pieces have repeating patterns. Some musicians see the patterns in colour. Mozart, for example."

"I love Mozart. All I ever wanted was to be a concert pianist. My mom bought me a baby grand and hired a 'renowned' teacher. But he wasn't too impressed. All he said was, 'Some children have the talent and some don't.' My mom didn't buy it. She told him my aunt was a concert pianist, so it's in my blood. She said, 'If Janine wants to be a concert pianist, then she will, if not with your help, with someone else's.' The next guy suggested I try a different piano; he knew of one for sale, a Steinway, and he could give her a good trade-in on the baby grand. Mom said to bring it over. The third guy told Mom my problem was that I watch my hands. And the fourth called me Miss Thumbs. My mom said, 'In her heart, she longs to be a concert pianist.' And he said, 'There is no heart that does not long.'"

"There is no heart that does not long." Dr. McCoy smiled at his student. "I like that. My topic with Byron Baird was neurocardiology studies at the Heart Mind Institute." Dr. McCoy paused while the waitress set down the two coffees and the third one with the scone. "In the processing of music, there are forty thousand music neurons in the heart, which are sending signals directly to the brain. That's the theory, anyway."

Janine nodded. "The heart–brain dialogue. The conscious mind is in the brain, but the subconscious is in the heart. I love that. In my heart, I longed to be a pianist, but my brain thought differently."

By the look of what was happening between these two, both student and teacher had longing in their hearts. I had heard there were rules now about liaisons between professors and students. But they probably weren't enforceable, like almost everything else nowadays. I had a long drive back to Broken Deer and I didn't want to waste time watching these two impressing one another. I leaned forward. "You either have the talent or you don't. Which is why I'm obsessed with the idea that this girl's talent not be wasted."

Dr. McCoy added sugar and a little cream, just enough to turn the black liquid murky, which was how I suddenly felt when Dr. McCoy asked, "What music program is she in now?"

"That's the problem. No program. While she was growing up, she worked with her grandfather, a fishing guide. Her synesthesia allowed her to read underwater currents, good for tracking fish." I laid my Zoom II4n, bought special for this occasion, on the table. "The last two years I've been paying her to clean the church, you know, mopping, sweeping, cleaning my apartment, that sort of thing. And she's been saving her money. She's old enough to leave the trailer park now. But where will she go? Then, like an answer to my prayers, I read in the paper that Juilliard is having an open competition in Toronto. But she needs a referral." I slid the audio recorder toward Dr. McCoy. "Would you like me to turn it on so you can hear her play?"

Dr. McCoy gestured to the other occupied tables. "I'd rather not listen here. But I can take it with me."

Janine looked confused. "She's a savant but her job is cleaning the church and catching fish? Does she own a piano at least?"

"She owns any piano she plays. But no, she plays the church piano."

Dr. McCoy said, "Owns any piano she plays. I like that."

Janine glanced from Dr. McCoy to me and back to Dr. McCoy. "But how did she learn to play?"

I knew the answer to this question. "She was born with it. It's like the music just happens."

"Happens," said Dr. McCoy. "I like that. Mozart's music happened, fell into his head as a synesthetic gestalt, full-blown in his brain, twenty minutes of music all in a flash. It took him months of hard labour to copy on paper this enormous tangle of sharps and flats and rhythms and tempos, which had *happened* in his brain in an instant of time."

"Amazing." Janine's elbows were on the table and she was leaning forward, her tank top breathlessly open for Dr. McCoy, who was looking into her eyes that were breathlessly blue.

He smiled a wide smile that wrinkled his crow's feet.

"You have a lovely smile," said Janine.

Dr. McCoy gave Janine's generous dimensions furtive glances as she added sugar to her coffee. Well, not very furtive. His thoughts were plain as day.

I cleared my throat. "You both have lovely smiles. But now—"

McCoy continued. "The Broken Deer girl. It's complicated, Janine. With you and me there are the notes, the keys, the fingers — all separate, all computed in different brain regions that come together and take form in the piano. Or look at it another way. Your nervous system sections the undifferentiated buzz of your surroundings into separate channels of sight, sound, smell, taste, and so on, sort of the way water and cream and sugar and coffee comes together and takes form in a cup. In other words, you're right now at this moment having an experience of the Red Brick café, which is a creation of your consciousness. Or stated simply, connections between brain modules that are distinct and functionally separate are experienced all at once.

"The savant sees the notes in colours, sometimes in their mind they see a colour-coded keyboard. But it can be a curse, depending on how you look at it — all these modalities of sound and sight and colour, normally perceptually separated, are triggered together in the brain of the savant as the result of cross-activation between adjacent brain regions, and you get not a savant like Michael Jackson but a savant like Rain Man. Or the man who could recite the players and the scores of every NBA game ever played but couldn't figure out how to use the remote to turn on the TV to watch an NBA game."

Dr. McCoy turned his attention to me. "I'm sorry. I'm giving a lecture. We were talking about the Broken Deer girl."

Janine sipped from her cup, her nail polish glinting in the overhead light as she set her coffee down. "I'm having trouble understanding this. She's a musical genius who works as a fishing guide and church cleaner."

Realizing my savant was starting to look like Rain Man with a job mopping floors, I tried again to explain. "You have to understand the situation. As well as not attending school, she had no family support. Her father drowned when she was a child, and her mother is an alcoholic. Nowhere near a Rain Man, if that's what you're thinking. This girl has amazing black eyes that seem able to see beyond what the rest of us can see, and hands even more amazing. Everything about her is amazing."

Dr. McCoy said, "I don't know about eyes, but I do know about hands." Dr. McCoy's head tipped back as he stepped into his stand and deliver: "For the gifted pianist, the left and the right play different notes simultaneously, up to twenty per second, one independent of the other, as though the left hand doesn't know what the right is doing. That is part of the savant's genius. If the pianist is concentrating on the individual notes and on the individual fingers of the individual hands finding the notes, she's playing the piano, yes, but not the music. The moment conscious mental factors leave the player is the moment the music begins to play. Hence the research now taking place in the Heart Mind Institute."

Janine interrupted. "Why do music savants usually play the piano?"

"At last, Janine, a question easily answered. The piano neatly divides the language system of music into a pattern of eighty-eight keys. It turns a savant's chaos of sense experience into a system of patterns they can control, which is why, once they discover the piano, they can't stop playing. Pattern intuition, it's called."

"You mean like ESP."

"Like ESP," I added. "You'll recognize that if you listen to the tape."

Dr. McCoy leaned forward. "Well, that's the theory — namely that, in advanced musical intelligence, some awareness functioning beyond conscious thought is happening. So for lack of a better word, Janine, ESP." He smiled a wide smile that wrinkled his crow's feet.

Janine's frown suggested she was still trying to make sense of it. "How can you have a new composition by the original composer, in this case Chopin, when the original composer is dead?"

I knew the answer to this one. "It's called acausal parallelism."

Dr. McCoy nodded. "I agree, Father, Carl Jung's theory of acausal parallelism. An interesting idea taken much more seriously now that the geneticists have discovered the DNA marker VMAT2, the gene that predisposes some individuals to spiritual or mystical transcendental capability."

Janine finished her coffee and put down her cup. "So, Father, she's a musical ESP genius who was born with a newly discovered gene that allows her to upload Chopin's consciousness."

"That is why I'm here."

Janine was scowling at her empty cup. "It has to be she plays by ear. Lots of people play by ear. If they hear it, they can play it."

McCoy explained. "To play by ear means you reproduce what you hear. But the true savant plays by instinct and imagination, from the heart, in other words. Savants give each piece a personal interpretation with completely unpredictable results. Pattern intuition is maybe a better word than ESP. In music there is an infinity of patterns that can be formed from eighty-eight keys. Sometimes two different people create identical patterns."

"Like ESP," I said. "You'll recognize that if you listen to this tape."

Dr. McCoy nodded. "When we listen to a true savant, we must keep in mind that the individual has often had no exposure to the actual notated music. But seat one at the piano and somehow, mystically, spookily almost, they create a completely new composition. So … yes. Like ESP."

"Exactly," I agreed. "So now if I could turn it on—"

"So every piece is not the one hundredth rendition of the original but a completely new composition of the original composer?" Janine's frown suggested she was still trying to make sense of it.

"Yes, exactly. So now if I could turn it on and—"

"Well, that's the theory. Namely that, in advanced musical intelligence, some awareness functioning beyond conscious thought is happening. So I suppose the result is a completely new composition by the original composer, so for lack of a better word, Janine, ESP. But I prefer pattern intuition."

"Exactly," I agreed. I slid the Zoom closer so that it was almost touching Dr. McCoy's cup.

Dr. McCoy did not pick up the Zoom. "I googled Broken Deer after you called me, Father. This little girl would have made a wonderful program for Byron Baird. Rent a helicopter, film an overhead of the area, miles of bush and lakes, and right in the middle, this mile-wide open area of scattered trailers — and then a zoom shot into the church basement, and there at the piano sits this little girl playing Chopin."

Janine's eyes sparkled as she added the write-up: "Out of one of the double-wides in this remote northern woods comes a seven-year-old musical genius."

I was overjoyed. "Exactly! But I don't want to make a movie. In fact, the land is all gravel pits now. But I do want a referral to the Juilliard competition."

Dr. McCoy frowned. He finished his coffee and set down the cup. He placed it squarely in front of me. "It's not that easy, Father. Referrals to Juilliard come from schools of music, gifted kids who've been in programs almost from birth."

"And I'm only the parish priest. And when I leave Broken Deer, I'll be leaving behind the most important part of my life. Her name is Aiyana. I always believed that when I left I'd take her with me. But how would that look? And take her to what? When my heart began to give up a few years ago, I prayed to the Angel of Mercy to keep me alive until I could get this girl into a music program. Years came and went with no answer from the Angel. Then a miracle happened. I noticed in the Sudbury library an article in the Globe and Mail written by Dr. Jerry McCoy, University of Toronto."

This statement seemed to catch Dr. McCoy's attention.

I added, "'Walkers Between Two Worlds.' That was the title."

Dr. McCoy explained. "I interviewed Keith Richards. He said he felt like a walking antenna: The music was out there, he just picked it up."

"Out there where?"

Dr. McCoy shrugged. "He meant, you know, a figure of speech."

"Keith Richards. Wow!"

I said, "Not a figure of speech, Dr. McCoy. You described him as a musical genius caught between the normal and the paranormal. One foot in this reality, the other in some other reality. He meant the other side."

"Wow!" said Janine.

I clasped my hands together in an involuntary gesture of hope. "Walker between worlds, the physical body walking with her alcoholic mother in Broken Deer, but her mind … walking with Chopin in symphonic heaven."

"Wow!" said Janine.

I turned to Dr. McCoy. "If ever I'm asked for an explanation for this girl, I have one word: *enhanced*."

"Enhanced," said Dr. McCoy. "Yes. Another good word."

Janine glanced from me to Dr. McCoy. "Like in that New Age Indigo Child stuff they talk about. Every so often a child already in our new stage of evolution is born into now." Janine reached for the recorder. "Let's turn it on."

"Yes," I agreed. "Finally. Let's turn it on."

But Dr. McCoy raised a hand. "I'm sorry, Father. I let this go as long as it did for Janine's sake. My guess is she's learned more from this conversation than she would from a semester of seminars." He sat back, distancing himself, it seemed, from his next pronouncement. "The truth is, savants have one thing in common: No one can understand them and they can't understand the neurosoup of activity bubbling in that three-pound mass of jelly called their brain. As children and as teenagers, they're frightened, confused, and alone. They survive by organizing their psychological chaos into OCD-type patterns. For this girl, her OCD is playing the piano."

I closed my eyes, trying to shut out the words.

But Dr. McCoy continued. "For people like her, solitude is often the only option. This is why they escape into their world of music, art, mathematics — whatever is their area of genius."

Dr. McCoy shifted his chair and stretched his legs in the tight jeans. "Without support from family, friends, teachers, or agents, savants usually self-destruct, which almost happened to Keith Richards and did happen to Michael Jackson."

Dr. McCoy slid the Zoom back to rest against my cup. "I don't want to take on the responsibility of a teenage OCD savant."

I slid it back to the middle of the table. "You won't have to. This is a very smart and very mature young woman. She's been forced to become strong and self-reliant. She won't self-destruct."

"In remote Ontario, no. I understand that, Father. But what will happen to her when she gets air-lifted out of the bush and dropped into the Juilliard School in New York City?"

I felt anger flush my face. "So we should just leave her in the trailer park? Is that what you're saying? Let her live out her life in the bush? Is that really what you're saying?"

"No, of course not. I'm saying you should try another approach."

"I can't accept that. I won't." I reached over to turn on the tape. But Dr. McCoy stopped me. For a moment both his hands were clasped over mine.

"I'm not interested in hearing the music, Father. It could be a recording of anyone; it's not admissible. And I don't buy the line about her never hearing Chopin. And this theory of acausal parallelism has never been proven."

Janine turned to Dr. McCoy. "What if he makes a video of her?"

At this suggestion, an idea surfaced, like a paranormal nudge from my Angel of Mercy, all this time hovering silently off to one side, ready to step in when needed. I took out my wallet. The photograph was a copy of the one I had framed for my bedside. I handed it to

Dr. McCoy. It had been taken a few weeks earlier. Aiyana was wearing faded jeans and a black top, her long black hair glistening in the afternoon sunlight in front of the church.

McCoy stared at the picture. He handed it to Janine.

She studied the photograph. "This is her? She's beautiful. What's she doing in a trailer park cleaning churches and catching fish? She's gorgeous."

McCoy took it back for another look.

"We can't just leave her there," said Janine. "You know the stories, raped and left in the ditch in the middle of winter to die. This girl is a movie star."

I reached over to turn on the player. But Dr. McCoy stopped me again. "I'll tell you what I'll do. Bring the girl to me and I'll listen to her play. We can get together in my apartment, put on a pot of coffee, and if I like what I hear and if I think I can arrange a support system for her, you and I can compose a letter to Juilliard."

Janine smiled.

Dr. McCoy took out a pen and wrote his address on his napkin.

I almost gave Janine a hug.

Dr. McCoy glanced at me. "Do you have email up there?"

"Not reliably. And I need a letter to show the mother. Send it to me by regular mail and I'll do the rest." I found a scrap of paper in one pocket and a pen in another. I scribbled on the paper, attempting to get the ink started. Dr. McCoy reached into his inner jacket pocket for one of his. The writing on the pen said Faculty of Music, University of Toronto. It felt like the Angel of Mercy had given me that pen to write down my Broken Deer address.

We stood and shook hands all around. Dr. McCoy said, "My last grad class is this evening, an end-of-semester party. But I'll do the letter first thing in the morning."

CHAPTER EIGHT

Aiyana

My letter from Dr. Jerry McCoy, Faculty of Music, University of Toronto, arrived, not that I could read it. But Father Clark, sitting across from me at the kitchen table in the church basement, read it to me three times.

"Give this to your mother. She might remember Skibo from when you were little. Tell her I've been saving up all these years in a special bank account. The piano fund, I call it. Every single night since you were a little girl, many of those nights sitting right here, I prayed to the Angel of Mercy to drop one of her feathers on this special child." He handed me a white feather. "It's happened. The same day I received this letter, I found this feather on the church step. So talk to your mother. Difficult, I know. Tell her I've already written Dr. McCoy and told him you're coming. He lives on Madison Avenue. It's a decent area. I lived in a room around the corner on St. George when I was a student at U of T."

"Where will I stay?"

"Dr. McCoy will look after that. I've included a cheque payable to him to cover your living expenses from now to the November fifth tryouts. Explain to your mother Juilliard is having scholarship auditions through the Toronto Symphony, and you have four months to get yourself ready, with Dr. McCoy's help."

"She'll say no."

"But we have to ask."

"But aren't you coming with me — to Toronto I mean?"

Father Clark took my hand. "Remember when you were seven years old and I would take this hand and say, 'I know how difficult your mother can be. But she needs you to help look after things.' Well, all that looking after things has made you strong. I think maybe that was the Angel's plan. You're old enough now to make your own decisions and strong enough to follow your dreams."

"But you have to come with me."

He tried to blink away the tears. "I'll be with you every step of the way, my child. But not in this body. I got my report from the cardiologists. The old ticker is very tired."

Father Clark looked at his watch. He got up and opened the cupboard in the corner. He stood at the counter mixing the two glasses of ginger ale, in each one an ice cube and one slice of lemon.

"Three o'clock," he said. "Let us give thanks to the Angel of Mercy."

So we sat with the ginger ale at the chrome-legged table and watched the fizzle of life's problems fade into nothing as its ice melted away and was gone, and then I took the lemon and put it on my tongue and closed my eyes and asked the Angel to please turn my life from sour to sweet, and then I drank the ginger ale.

CHAPTER NINE

Eric

When I moved into the main-floor apartment in the old Wilson house on Madison Avenue — a quiet, tree-lined, inner-city street with turn-of-the-century two- and three-storey brick houses, much like the street I grew up on in Boston — Hilda, a retired nurse, lived on the second floor. Hilda's manicured grey hair and pear-shaped body reminded me of Miss Pinch, my grade-three teacher at Boston Private.

"I've just accepted a five-year contract with the IRS branch office in Toronto auditing American mining companies," I told her.

Hilda's hand was short and pudgy, but I did manage with my big hand a sort of handshake. She said, "You've come from a dystopia into a utopia. I suggest you marry a nice Canadian girl and become a citizen."

The next day she introduced me to Julia, a freelance nature journalist.

Four years later, here I was, seated in Julia's apartment, ready to ask the nice Canadian girl the question. Julia had made a chicken dinner. Very nice. I lived on microwave warm-ups for supper.

"Peonies," said Julia, nodding to the vase sitting in the centre of the table. "They're a springtime symbol of universal unifying power. I sold that series of articles to Cottage Life. The next series will be on the mystical power of different indigenous flowers. The one after that will be about the healing power of the lowly dandelion. The yellow flower is a sun symbol: When the warm spring sun coaxes the honeybees out of hibernation, their first food source is the dandelion. And I'm still trying to finish my article on anti-cremation."

"What's wrong with cremation?"

"Burning the body into a bag of ashes interferes with the natural transformative process and prevents the spirit from moving to the next level. It's not natural. We consume the cow, the cow consumes the grass, the grass consumes the fallen leaves, the leaves return to the earth and from the earth comes the grass for the cows to consume in spring. That is the natural order of things."

She got up and began to tidy the dishes. "In other words, Eric, the reason I'm telling you this, my articles are all overdue. I need a good chunk of writing time in my cabin to get them finished."

No surprise there. Julia's articles were always overdue. Her credit cards were usually maxed out. That was why I'd never been to her cabin. She went alone with her laptop to catch up on her work. And that was why, although I loved her completely and wanted to marry her, her free-spirit nature had held me back. As an accountant, I needed things to be organized and on time with dates set down and figures added up and everything tidied into its proper place — unlike Julia's apartment, which was packed with antiques that had belonged to her parents: a dresser, a china cabinet, a chesterfield with matching stuffed chairs. On top of the piano sat three stacks of old '78 vinyl LPs. Next to the piano, on an end table, sat an old turntable. The classical LPs and the old turntable would be a real find for someone, but I was tone-deaf, so music held no interest for me.

But I was interested in seeing her cabin. "The weekend is going to be warm, even for May. Maybe you'll finally let me come for a day or two."

She poured the after-dinner coffee and sat opposite me. "I'm short on time, as usual. How about an overnight before I start my two weeks on my own, no interruptions."

"Fine with me." Then I asked, "How long a drive is it?"

"About four hours to get to the Lost Loon Lakes." Julia got up and went into the kitchen for cream and sugar. She came back wearing a smile. "An overnight road trip. Sounds romantic. I can't wait!"

I think she sensed what I was planning. She seemed to have a sixth sense, like ESP.

She said, "The ice has been out since mid-April so the water will be warming up. We leave early, go in by canoe, build a fire, roast hot dogs for lunch, and stop at Weber's for hamburgers next day on the way back."

Now I hesitated. "By canoe? Can't we get there by motorboat?"

"It's too remote. Besides, I don't have a motorboat. The canoe's a family heirloom. It comes with a story. Do you want to hear it?"

I shrugged. Julia had all kinds of nature stories. I was used to that.

"My Grandpa Buster bought the cabin from a trapper who'd paddle in using an old sixteen-foot cedar strip and stay the winter to work his trapline. One January, he wanted to go home to see his wife, but there was three feet of snow and no way out. So he asked God — he was a Catholic, you know, and he called God the Boss. 'Boss,' he said, 'will you fly me home in my canoe to see my wife?' So the Boss said, 'Yes, if you promise not to fly that heavy cedar strip over any of my Catholic churches.' So the trapper got in the canoe and the Boss lifted him into the sky, and off he went, careful not to paddle over any Catholic churches. But then it got stormy and he couldn't see and he flew over a Catholic church. The Boss dropped him out of the sky and that was the end of the trapper. So when Grandpa Buster heard the story from the trapper's wife, he asked if he could buy the cabin. She said, 'Okay, but you have to clean up what's left of the cedar strip, which is still in the churchyard.'"

"And that's how you got your canoe?"

"A Grumman isn't a cedar strip. But yes, sort of. The Grumman was left at the cabin."

Well okay, a nice story, told in a typical Julia way, as though she actually believed it was true. That's how a writer's mind worked, it seemed, fantasy and reality often interchangeable. Which was okay with me. After four years together, I'd learned that her romantic personality complemented my sometimes overly rigid accountant personality and gave me a healthier balance. So, if at twenty-nine proposing to Julia was what I finally decided to do, what better place than in a romantic cabin on a secluded lake?

I marked the date on my calendar in my office and in my day planner, printed in bold and highlighted in yellow: Propose to Julia. Printed in bold in my mind were variations of the question I would need to ask to make it sound like an offhanded suggestion, in case she turned me down. Plan ahead. Cover your bases. You never know.

...

Looking healthy, tanned, and radiant, Julia arrived at my apartment at 5:00 a.m., right on time. I was not quite ready, because I expected her to be late. I pulled on my jacket, the ring tucked away in one pocket. Julia followed me along the hall, through the outer door, down three steps, and across the street to my Wrangler. We'd fastened the canoe to the carrier the day before. The trip north to the Loon Lakes was four hours up the 400 in the direction of Sudbury. Julia had brought her favourite CDs and played Chopin on my Wrangler Kicker audio system all the way to Sideroad 15, where she shut down the Kicker.

"Make a sharp left onto this gravel cut-off. It used to be a logging road so it's pretty rough. All these gravel roads up here are full of potholes and have blind sharp curves, none of them marked."

We parked in a clearing and carried Julia's fifteen-foot Grumman to the rocky shoreline of Little Lost Loon Lake. She slid the canoe into the water and I held it while she returned to the Wrangler for the supplies, which amounted to one canvas bag containing a few groceries, and a second one with what looked like her laptop. I had some overnight stuff in a backpack.

With one fluid motion, Julia slipped into the canoe and settled in the front. I managed to fit one foot, then the other, into the tippy bottom. Then, one hand on each side after manoeuvring out of an impossible tangle of legs and trousers and feet, I managed to sit upright.

She said, "Your first time in a canoe. Should we change places?"

"I'll be fine. I'll get the hang of it." Meaning if I tried to stand up to switch I'd end up in the lake.

I got myself organized and we shoved off. Julia waited patiently as I sorted out the moves with the paddle. Not only did the canoe want to go left when I paddled on the right, it wanted to go right when I paddled on the left.

The next problem: She said we'd stop on the shoreline for lunch. I hoped we'd find a spot with a log like a bench to sit on so as not get grass stains on my pants, but more than that, I feared I wouldn't be able to get up from my seat without falling overboard. After thirty minutes paddling, I noticed a reedy inlet with a flock of ducks swimming around. Needing to uncramp my legs, I said, "Can we stop in that little inlet for a break?"

But then another problem: To get out of the canoe in this particular spot would mean stepping into the water in my new hundred-dollar MEC runners. Not a problem for Julia, who was up and off the end and on the shore without even a splash. I picked my tippy way to the front, hands sliding along the sides of the canoe. I stepped out and sloshed through the water.

Julia watched me with a quirky smile. "The first time Grandpa Buster and I canoed the Mattawa River, we tipped three times. Then we did the Rollway Rapids on the Petawawa. Same canoe, with no tipping. You get used to it."

A stroke of luck. There was a flat rock to sit on not far from the ducks that were looking at me, quacking and flapping, laughing at me for being incompetent.

Julia leaned forward to pick a blade of grass. "Buster would say, according to Indigenous legend, the Boss's two favourite colours are green and blue. Grass and trees, water and sky."

The ducks began a round of squawks. The racket took my mind from the green of the grass to the blue of the water to my first day at school, squirming and clutching myself at my desk, afraid to ask the teacher if I could go to the washroom. Here I was, a twenty-nine-year-old, feeling shaky from that tippy teetering canoe, needing to ask to go to the washroom. "Um … I have to find a washroom."

"Go in the woods."

Simple as that. Except that the woods were full of black flies and mosquitoes.

She watched me swat my way back to the rock. She handed me a spray bomb of bug repellent. She asked, "Do you want a beer and something from the cooler? Or we can go all the way to the cabin. The bugs will eat us alive if we stay here."

"Let's go to the cabin. That is, as long as I can get back into that canoe without losing my mind in the mud."

"I'll help you. This time you ride in front."

"I need a canoe for beginners."

In one fluid motion, she climbed in. Having learned a few tricks from the last time, I grasped the gunwales to maintain balance and managed a not-too-tippy boarding. I knelt in the bow and settled myself on my haunches. This time Julia tossed me a life jacket.

"I'm a good swimmer," I reminded her. "I was on the Harvard swimming team."

"It doesn't matter. From here on can be dangerous. The wind can come out of nowhere and churn this lake into whitecaps. And the water this far out is freezing, thirty feet of melted ice. I carry my rosary beads for this stretch just in case."

Rosary beads? I knew she was a practising Catholic but I'd never seen her with rosary beads. I thought they were for a near-death thing. But although the lake was flat as a mirror, we were completely isolated, the bush growing right up to the water's edge with no sign of civilization anywhere. I fastened my life jacket. By the time we were halfway across the open stretch, I'd perfected the paddle technique and felt competent, although I wished I had a more comfortable seat.

At ten past two we arrived at the board-framed loggers cabin, a square box with an open porch across the front. As we eased the canoe against the plank dock jutting out from a shoreline of flat black rocks, Julia reached into the shallows to pick up a white feather.

"If you find one that's floated into shore, it means the angels are with you. To prove it, they leave a white feather in your path."

Angels and rosary beads. Well, so what. Nothing wrong with being a good Catholic. I was raised Catholic, was an altar boy in fact, but for me church ended when high school began. But I'd have no trouble going back to the church.

As I followed her up the path to the front door, she pointed to a patch of white flowers. "Those are trilliums. The symbol of the balance between the material and the spiritual. Another one of my articles."

The cabin was not locked; I guessed she'd lost the key. Inside was quaint and cozy: two tiny bedrooms, a living room with a stone fireplace, and a small kitchen with a wood-burning cookstove.

She set her laptop on the table. "I try to remember to back everything up on my external hard drive but I sometimes forget. Half the time I don't know where it is. The hazards of a laptop freelancer..."

"But you seem organized when it comes to wilderness stuff."

She stopped laying supplies on the table. She seemed to be thinking about what I'd said. "Here the rules are different. The importance is different. There's no cellphone coverage. Even if you have a landline, the ambulance service is limited, so 911 is unreliable. You're entirely on your own. The closest community is Broken Deer, but apart from a disgusting trailer park, the whole town is boarded up."

I looked around. The furniture was old, the unpainted board walls were covered with outdoor paraphernalia: snowshoes, canoe paddles, stuffed fish mounted on plaques, fishing rods, cross-cut logging saws.

She opened a kitchen cupboard and pulled out a Canadian flag. "The first thing Buster did every spring was raise the flag."

From the front step, I watched her fasten the rope to a wooden pole by the dock. I thought only Americans flew flags. I thought Canadians couldn't care less about flags. Guess not.

While Julia prepared a salad and cold ham for supper — she'd scrapped the hot dog idea — I braved the icy water for a swim. My canoe experience had made me feel like an incompetent sissy. I hoped she'd be watching as I waded to my knees and pushed off across the flat surface. I breaststroked until the cold choked off my lungs, forcing me back to shore before Julia noticed.

Julia opened a bottle of wine. We sat in folding lawn chairs at the shoreline to eat supper. That is until the bugs drove us inside. As we were finishing and dusk was falling, two loons began to call from opposite ends of the lake.

Julia said, "It's a spooky call until you know what they're saying. *Where are you? Where are you?*" She set her glass down. "They mate for life. Like people used to."

She was nudging me into the question, already sensing my plan with her ESP, giving me a little help. "This is an amazingly romantic spot," I said, working up to it.

"If I don't have children to pass the cabin on to, that could be the end of the cabin."

She wasn't just giving me a nudge; she was almost asking me. She said, "Can you make a fire while I set up the bed?"

I knew enough to lay out the paper and place the wood on top. But the paper flared up for ten seconds and went out. She came over and dismantled the wood and crumpled the paper and added the twigs and sat down on the chesterfield. Now, in front of the snap and crackle, the perfect time. Except that — I don't know, first the canoe incompetence, then the fire incompetence, add to that I had managed only five minutes in the water — I was feeling even more like an incompetent sissy.

But I put the feeling aside. I settled onto the couch, Julia beside me saying, "When I was a kid, Buster and Ida — she's still in the hospital, by the way — we would light the fire and play Trivial Pursuit. My grandma always won; she was very smart."

Another possibility. We could play Trivial Pursuit and then, when it was my turn to ask her a question, I'd say, "Will you marry me?"

"When I was fifteen, Buster and I flew to James Bay and canoed the Moose River fur-trade route to Lake Superior. I wrote it up and it got published. That's how I got into journalism."

"What did Buster do for a living?"

"He was a forest ranger. But not a policeman type. He was easygoing. Everyone loved him. He proposed to Ida in a flat-bottom bass boat sitting in the weeds on Big Deer River. Ida knew he liked apple pie so she baked him one, her first try at baking. When Buster took a bite, he almost choked. But he didn't want to say anything because he was going to propose. So when Ida was distracted by two loons making a fuss along the shore, he slipped his pie over the edge into the weeds. Ida took a bite of the pie and said, 'This is terrible.' But Buster said, 'Tasted good to me.' So Ida knew he was a good catch and said yes before he even asked her."

When the loons called again, Julia said, "One will be at one end of the lake, the other on the opposite shore or in a bay somewhere." She glanced at me before imitating the rhythm of the call, *Where are you? Where are you?*

She might as well have been saying, Why are you taking so long to say four small words?

I was about to, when she said, "I'm exhausted. I think it's time for bed."

Too late. I would try again tomorrow, noting as I undressed, that the bed was not a double, not even a decent single, some sort of homemade arrangement with a lumpy mattress. But because of the fresh air and the swim, I no sooner climbed under the covers than I was asleep.

When I woke up next morning, Julia was already busy at the crackling wood stove, the coffee percolating, the bacon frying. An early morning fog was hanging over the lake. I sat at the kitchen table leafing through an old Outdoor Canada magazine while Julia made bacon and eggs in a black iron skillet. She toasted bread on the stove's surface. We did the dishes in water pumped from the lake and heated to boiling in an old kettle, Julia washing, me drying. Now the sun coming up over the flat blue lake was slanting through the fog, making ghostly patterns on the cabin's front window that seemed to be saying, If you don't hurry and ask, you'll miss your chance. Four small words. How hard could that be?

Julia wrung out her cloth and hung it on a hook above the sink. "Can I show you my photo albums? Other peoples' albums are boring, so I won't make you look at too many."

We sat at the kitchen table and looked through the photos, all of Julia and Ida and Buster. One album was variations of little Julia: standing on the shoreline, leaning over, peering down at a turtle or a frog or a rabbit. Another picture was of a bigger Julia, holding up a fish, the notations on the back reading "Julia at eight," "Julia at ten," and so on. Other pictures showed an adult Julia camping with Buster: pitching the tent, standing in front of the tent, taking down the tent. The last picture was of Julia sitting on the front step of the cabin.

She pulled a second album across the old wooden table and flipped it open. "These are from a portage trip into Broken Deer Lake."

One photo in particular caught my attention. Julia stood on the shoreline looking over the water, watching something. The flat black rocks at Broken Deer Lake looked almost identical to those right outside the cabin.

"The stone game," Julia explained. "You pick a stone with lots of colours and stand near the shore and make a wish. Then you throw the stone and watch the circles form into an angel and leave the surface, taking the wish with her. But it's not just throwing any old stone. You have to find the stone with colours that speak to you and then you make a wish and then you focus your mind on the colours in the stone and then you throw, not too far out, but far enough that the circles can spread and not break on the shore. That's very important. If you break the circles, no angel will form. And you can't tell anyone your wish. The wish is between you and the angel. Telling someone will break the circles, and the opposite of the wish will come back to haunt you. Come on, I'll show you."

The fog had become heavier, so thick along the shoreline that she had to take my hand and lead me, picking up stones along the path to the water. She held one in her hand and gently rubbed the surface with her finger. "Broken Deer Lake has amazing stones. But these are okay. The fluorites are the blues; the reds are iron oxide, quartz too. These are good colours."

She scooped up a few more and held her palm open toward me. I picked one about two inches across, perfectly round. She picked one that was almost the same. "It's a bit foggy, but we can still see the water. Don't forget: You have to concentrate on the stone, and you can't just do an ordinary throw with an ordinary plunk. You have to visualize the angel carrying the wish and leaving the water as the circle leaves the water. The angels speak to us quietly, in silent coincidences and in small tugs. You just have to listen."

I swung my right arm back and to the side, ready to throw — and stopped. "I want to tell you my wish."

Julia spun toward me. "No! You can't. If you tell me, it'll break the circle and the angel will turn the wish back on you."

"But I have to tell you before we leave. That was my plan. I tried to tell you last night but—"

"Eric, no, you can't."

I leaned back again and this time threw the stone, which landed about ten feet out. I waited for the circles to spend themselves. Then I turned to Julia. "I wish to marry you."

Julia dropped her stone. It rolled a few feet and settled on the shoreline. She covered her face with her hands. "Marry me? You shouldn't have told me! Now it won't come true."

She turned and marched back to the cabin.

"It's just a silly game!" I called. "Of course it'll come true."

Julia flapped a hand in the air, batting my words away. She disappeared into the cabin. I turned back to the lake, my head as foggy as the shoreline. A few minutes later, the screen door slammed. Julia trudged down the path, two bags in her arms. She climbed into the canoe and sat there with her arms crossed.

I sighed and followed.

We crossed the lake in silence through the dense fog. Without a word, we loaded the canoe onto the Wrangler and set off along the gravel sideroad. By this time the fog was closing in so thick and so heavy I couldn't see beyond the headlights.

When we turned off the bush road onto Sideroad 15, the fog began to lift so I picked up speed.

Julia sat up straight. "Slow down before the next turn." Her voice was a flat and sullen order.

I snapped back, "It was only a stupid game. You don't worry about maxing out your credit card and missing deadlines and losing your keys but you go ballistic about a silly game."

I upped the speed.

"The turns are bad here, Eric."

"Some silly childhood superstition and then all of a sudden it's a big deal." I upped the speed. "It was a big deal for me. I've been planning it for months."

"Slow down! This is a bad one."

I felt the wheels of the Wrangler pull into a sideways slide on the gravel. We hit the shoulder with a jolt and rolled once before landing on all four wheels, the headlights burning twin beams through the low-lying patches of pea-soup fog. My heart racing, my fingers clutching the steering wheel, I remembered my conversation with the car salesman who had shown me the roll bars and told me these Wranglers were built like tanks. I said to Julia, "These Wranglers are built like tanks."

When she didn't answer I glanced at her. She was slumped sideways, held upright by her seat belt. I called her name, touched her hand, but she didn't move. I unbuckled, climbed out, and ran to her side of the Wrangler. I opened her door and eased her limp body out of its harness. Finding no wounds, I picked her up and settled her in the grass ten feet in front of the vehicle to examine her under the headlights. But they glared too high and too bright, straight into my eyes and into the fogged-in fields. When I knelt and gently nudged her shoulder, her right hand reached up and gripped my arm.

I placed my hand over hers. "You're okay. No cuts. Nothing broken. Just a knock on the head. I'm going to call an ambulance to get you checked out."

I tried to move away, but her fingers tightened and squeezed into my muscle. Then she turned her head and said something. I leaned down but couldn't make out the words. She tried again, her voice a whisper: "Where are you?" The fingers of her cold hand contracted around my arm in one final spasm before releasing their grip. Her arm fell to her side.

I gently set her head down on the grass and ran back to the Wrangler. I turned off the too-bright headlights, retrieved my cellphone from the glove compartment, and dialled 911. As I hurried back to her, my eyes searched through the wisps of fog along the wire fence running along the edge of a field of uncut corn, trying to find a landmark. The corn was watching me, it seemed, its leaves whispering in voices of accusation. My gaze shifted to a sign on the opposite side of the road. I told the dispatcher we were at a sharp corner on Sideroad 15 next to a cornfield, opposite the Broken Deer sign. "We must be coming to a crossroads because the sign says Little Lost Loon Lake to the left and Broken Deer Lake to the right. I think. It's hard to tell. The sign is full of bullet holes."

"It'll be at least thirty minutes. Is she conscious?"

"I don't think so."

"Does she have a pulse?"

My heart stopped. "Oh … I-I'm sure she does."

"You'd better check."

With trembling fingers I searched, first her wrist then her throat. Nothing. I searched her body for breaks or cuts, something to fix, but could find nothing, no blood to stop, no wound to patch. All I could find was the white feather, stuck in the back pocket of her jeans.

I sobbed into the phone, "I can't find anything. No pulse, no wounds, no breaks. What happened?"

"It's probably blunt-force trauma. Don't move her. Wait for the ambulance."

"I've already moved her."

"Well don't. Stay with her but don't move her."

I sat beside her, holding the feather, thinking I shouldn't have moved her. I could see her picking up the feather, saying, "You broke the wish, Eric. The Angel has turned her back on you, and this is what has happened."

I buried my face in my arms, tears rolling down my face. I felt the fingers of the cold breeze that had been muttering in the corn begin to creep up my back. I saw beyond the cornfield a line of trees shrouded by the fog. On the other side of these trees? I didn't know what lay on the other side. I didn't understand why I would wonder about the other side. On the other side was probably another gravel road leading to another bush and another lake.

I didn't move until the police car came around the corner and then the ambulance, sirens screaming and hazard lights flashing and headlights flooding the fog-covered road. Two paramedics stepped out. A pyramid of white arched through the fog, across the grass, along the line of corn, to settle for a moment on a patch of wildflowers before sliding along the fence until it finally found Julia. The light covered her with a steady white glare that faded into pale as the paramedic approached.

"I think you got here too late," I said, already trying to blame someone besides myself.

I noticed the pieces of the canoe strewn along the roadside. I saw an O.P.P. cruiser pull up. I watched the paramedics examining Julia.

"What's her name?"

"Julia."

I watched the paramedic open the waistband of her jeans to feel along her stomach cavity. Then he felt her wrist. "Hold on, hold on. I've got a pulse." He knelt closer. "Julia, can you hear me? Sudbury General is half an hour away. Hang on. We'll be there in no time."

I heard the policeman's boots slap-slap in a heavy plod through the wet grass to stop next to Julia. But the paramedics needed no help to slip her onto the stretcher and into the ambulance. They left, sirens wailing.

I was alone with the big-bellied bulk of the policeman who was staring at the Wrangler. "I need to see your registration and driver's licence."

I gave them to him.

"You're driving with an American licence."

"I'm here on a work visa."

The policeman returned the papers.

"Those Wranglers are easy to roll. They're built too high up."

"The salesman didn't tell me."

The policeman pulled in his belly and hiked up his pants. "Maybe you shouldn't have moved her."

"I know, I know. But I was looking for cuts, gashes. I have a first-aid kit."

The policeman tipped back his hat, scowling at me, waiting for a confession of guilt, it seemed.

I confessed. "I don't know. I was confused, in shock. I didn't know what to do."

"Your vehicle registration gives your address as Madison Avenue in Toronto. What brings you up here?"

"Julia has a cabin on Lost Loon Lake. We were doing a quick overnight and then back to Toronto."

"Your first time up here?"

"Yes. I—"

"You don't know the roads up here."

"No."

"Driving that Wrangler too fast on gravel roads, the stones work like ball bearings."

"I'm sorry." My shoulders slumped, my head bowed. "I'm so sorry."

"I can phone for a tow into Sudbury. I can give you a ride to the hospital."

As we were climbing into the cruiser, the policeman's cellphone rang. He talked briefly. He slipped his hand into an inner pocket, produced a pen, and made a note in his pad.

I didn't know what the policeman wrote with that pen but I did know what the angels wrote with the pointed end of that feather. Time of death: 1:00 p.m. May 24, 2021.

CHAPTER TEN

Aiyana

I was standing in the unusual hot May sun in front of Harry's. Hartley's mile-long Caddy pulled up on the gravel shoulder. Hartley got out and walked around to the passenger side while I climbed into the driver's seat and slipped the Caddy into gear. We drove to the top end of the lake where the road crossed the Broken Deer River and curved up to a high cliff. We practised parking at the fire lookout tower. Then we drove to the Visitor Information Centre and practised back-in parking. Hartley took some pictures.

As we curved down through the bush toward the trailer park at the bottom I began to feel something wasn't right. I eased back on the gas pedal as the road graded down toward the church. I stopped the car. Off in the distance, the rows of aluminum-clad double-wides shone in the sunlight. Closer up, near Harry's Groceries and Bait, where the road levelled off, the backhoes were tearing up the gravel. All that looked the same.

I turned off the car.

"What's the matter?" asked Hartley.

"I don't know. I'm feeling something, like echoes I shouldn't be hearing, because I'm too far out of earshot."

The weigh station at the gravel works looked the same. Nearer the bridge, where the river ran slow and deep, currents were shimmering like blue silk in the sun, the same as always. My eye followed the blue curve, where the river ran into the lake and dropped into an underwater current thirty feet deep. In the sun, this current stretched out in shades of green and indigo almost to the lake's centre. That was the same.

Far off to the right, a black lab was standing at the edge of one of the pits. "That's Father Clark's dog. Why isn't he at the church?"

Hartley frowned. "Why should he be? He's a dog."

"He's hearing something. Something's not right."

But everything looked normal. A truck turned into the pits and stopped. A man in a berry-and-rust plaid jacket driving a front-end loader scooped up the gravel, the silver sparkle in the stone covered now with dust as, raising the shovel, the machine scooted back to the truck to dump into the waiting box, back and forth, until the truck was loaded and another took its place.

Then Farley turned and looked straight at me. He couldn't see me, of course, but I could see him.

I opened the car door. "I have to go to the church."

"When do we go driving again?"

"Never."

"What? Why not?"

"My mother doesn't like it."

"I'll drive you to the church."

"I'll cut across the field. It's quicker."

I found Father Clark in his church apartment shivering on his couch. I covered him with his blanket. I slipped off my jean jacket, pulled up a chair, and sat down beside him. He reached out for the white feather and an elastic band sitting next to him on the end table. "The Angel has been waiting for you. It's time." With shaky fingers, he fastened the feather to one long strand of my hair. He touched the feather. "The Angel is with you, Aiyana, and so am I, so now it's time."

I covered him with a second blanket. I mixed two ginger ales. I held his glass for him. "Like the ice cube, Father, cold for a few minutes and then melted and gone. Like the slice of lemon, Father, sour for a few minutes" — I used the stir stick to fish the lemon from the glass — "then turned to sweet."

His hands were so shaky I had to hold them quiet as I helped him put the lemon on his tongue. Then I put the lemon on my tongue. I felt it turn my taste from sour to sweet, and I watched his lemon turn his taste from sour to sweet. "And now what's left, Father, is the ginger ale, which by drinking will take away the shiver and the fizzle and the sour of life, and you will be warm." I helped him drink his ginger ale and then I drank my ginger ale and then I saw that he was warm.

Even if I had run to Harry's and had him phone 911, I already knew that both 911 and the ambulance were busy with someone else because, from the way Farley had been acting, I knew he was hearing another ambulance, wondering why it was going in the other direction.

It didn't matter. I knew he didn't want me to phone 911, even if I could dial the numbers right. I knew he didn't want to be taken by ambulance to spend his last hours in Sudbury General suspended between this side and the other side by tubes that would do nothing except add a day or two. Don't let them delay my exit, he told me. That's how he said it. I knew all he wanted was for me to sit with him each day that he had left so that I would be with him to mix the ginger ale, so together we could watch this day's fizzle fade away and this day's ice melt into gone and this day's sickness turn from sour to sweet.

I picked up Socks and left the church, nowhere for either of us to go. With Father Clark gone the church would be gone, and the church piano would be gone. "But now," I heard myself say it out loud to the angel, "I'll be gone too, with or without my mother's permission."

Two gravel guys standing outside Harry's called and whistled as I walked into the store. "Hey, bush bait, what's with the feather?" I went up to the counter, my back to the door. The two men outside were talking and swearing, shouting at their buddies in the gravel trucks rumbling by on their way to weigh-in.

Harry said, "I'll look after it, Aiyana. Go out the back door so they don't bother you. I'll go over to the church myself and we'll get it looked after together."

I turned toward home, well, not home, my mother's double-wide. Father Clark had been my home, not windows and porches, but feelings and connections, essences maybe. Like in the old days Grandpa Willie talked about, before seventeen-year-old girls wore jean jackets and walked gravel roads with their long hair swinging behind them and their butts swaying them to Harry's where the gravel guys standing outside called and whistled and made comments about bush-bait trailer-park trash and then took them to the drive-in.

CHAPTER ELEVEN

Eric

The hospital told me Julia's grandmother was too ill to receive calls or visitors, especially not a message that her granddaughter had been killed. I asked them to contact me if her situation improved. No doubt Ida would eventually ask for Julia, and I wanted to be the one to tell her.

I searched Julia's apartment but could find no personal papers other than household bills and two overdue credit card statements. Then I remembered her laptop. I'd emptied the Wrangler before it was towed away. No laptop there. Maybe it was in the ditch.

The undertaker from the MacNamara Funeral Home on Yonge Street suggested a notice online and in the newspaper: visitation two to four and seven to nine and then cremation. I knew Julia wouldn't like the idea of cremation. It wasn't natural. It wasn't back to the earth. It was violent. I asked Father Hankey. He assured me that most people wanted cremation and that most religions saw it as the release of the spirit from the body. Julia would like that part, he said. I thought, no, Julia would not want her spirit released from a crematorium chimney.

But, my mind by this time reeling, I agreed.

During afternoon visitation, I introduced myself to the few individuals who came to pay their respects. Julia's bulky, balding landlord with his heavy accent said, "Who will remove Julia's things from the apartment?"

"I'll look after everything," I said. "But it'll take time. The piano belonged to her grandmother, the furniture was from her parents. Her relatives will want those things. Can I leave them there for now and pay the rent?"

"Sorry. I've already booked the painters, and I have a waiting list for that apartment. And Julia was two months behind on her rent."

"I'll look after it."

Visitors from her church came and went, but none knew of any relatives. At the service in the funeral parlour, Father Hankey said some nice words about God's will, a pleasant way of rationalizing what was either bad luck or negligence, depending on your point of view. I wished I could have chosen either God's will or bad luck but I knew I'd be stuck with negligence.

At the end of the service, Hilda from the upstairs apartment said, "I overheard the conversation with Julia's landlord. I've had my name on the list for a retirement unit. If I don't take it, my name drops off the list, so I'm moving at the end of next week. There's still almost two months left on my apartment. You can store Julia's things there."

Dropped off the list. That's how I felt. What list? My list. The list I had already made of things to do with Julia. The list of events I would write on my calendar to go to with Julia. Now I had nothing on my calendar and nothing I wanted to write on it, other than a reminder to have the movers pack her things and put them into Hilda's one-bedroom.

When the movers ran out of room at Hilda's, I told them to put the end table, recliner, two lamps, cabinet, and piano into my living room. I moved her dresses and winter coats into my closet. Now my apartment was so crowded I could barely move. I telephoned all the names in the guest book from the funeral home, thinking I might not have asked every visitor about her connections. But no cousin or uncle or aunt was found. Then I realized I shouldn't have stored everything before making a more thorough search for her laptop or her personal papers, like an envelope tucked away somewhere. Without a will, her estate would be frozen for months. I searched through every drawer but found nothing but dishes and tea towels and napkins and, of course, all her clothes.

A week later, I received a call from the funeral home saying the ashes, now resting in a black urn, were ready for pick up. Then I received a call from Ida. Her voice was shaky. "I'm so sorry, Eric. I didn't know. They didn't tell me until just this minute."

"It's under control. When you're ready for visitors, I'll drop by."

"One thing. Could you sprinkle her ashes at the cabin?"

"Of course."

"Cast them over the water from the dock. That's what we did with Buster. She'll want to be with Buster."

"Are there other relatives I can contact?"

"Oh, somewhere … but we lost touch long ago."

...

Two weeks after Julia's death, I cancelled her subscriptions to the magazines she wrote for, which were now being sent by her former landlord to my address. Other reminders of Julia appeared in my apartment: a hairpin on the floor, an earring on the night table, a sock under the bed. If only I could get her stuff tidied away, I could get on with my life.

But Julia had also left herself in the form of fully lit technicolor recollections springing up in front of me so vivid they gave me chills: standing by the kitchen counter in jean cut-offs arranging wildflowers in blues and greens and reds and yellows, sitting on the edge of the bed in a halter top and shorts fastening her white sandals, sitting with her back to me in the bow of the canoe watching the loons. And the most frequent of all, the wish game, its memory logging time in my mind as though those two stones were sitting in the black container with her ashes, now resting on my bookshelf, catching my eye every time I passed.

By the end of July, eight weeks after the accident, the unbidden reminders had stopped appearing and the magazines had stopped arriving. As the memories faded, my mind was left with gaps, like empty pages in a book, like a Lang calendar with blank dates, like a vase with no flowers.

I took out photos I had found in a box in her apartment of a canoe trip through the Broken Deer Lakes with Buster. I put them on the coffee table to look through when I had nothing else to do. I'd ask her, "Which Deer Lake were you at in this picture?" And I'd look up the location on my laptop. When I caught myself talking to her out loud, I'd turn around, for a moment convinced she was in the room with me.

One day a call from the lawyer confirmed that Julia's only living relative was her grandmother. So I began the job of going through Julia's things, piece by piece, box by box, item by item. And as I did, vague sightings of my Julia came flooding back, as though her unbidden spirit, not released through cremation, was living in the urn.

I sat in my living-room recliner — in fact in Julia's recliner — and tried to put together a plan. I began a list. The furniture would continue to haunt me until I got rid of it. Because the piano took so much space, it would be the priority. I phoned various music stores. No one was interested in an old piano. As I sat in the recliner staring at the urn, my mind going in spooky circles, I realized that the piano, like the urn, had a shiny black finish. I got up and put the urn on the piano. It was a perfect match. It was like having a suit jacket in one hand and a tie in the other and trying them on in the mirror together and, ah, a perfect match.

Perhaps I should keep the piano. I could keep half her ashes on the piano and take the other half to the cabin. This thought led to a question. How would I get the ashes to the cabin? I would not go by canoe alone. I didn't know how to drive a motorboat even if I could rent one. I opened my laptop and searched Lost Loon Lake but there were no boat-taxi listings.

CHAPTER TWELVE

Aiyana

I sat on the bottom porch step of our double-wide. Sunday. No gravel trucks rumbling past throwing up dust. But right now dust was not my problem. Yesterday, I had shown Dr. McCoy's letter to my mother. She read it and stuck it in the kitchen cupboard and said, "No."

I held the cold glass of orange juice against my forehead, wishing it was ginger ale so I could listen to the hissing of the bubbles fizzing into nothing and the crackling of the ice melting into gone. Then I would ask the Angel of Mercy to help me figure out how to leave this ugly trailer park for good, with or without my mother's approval. I would say to the Angel, "Please send me a plan." But not in writing.

Cigarette smoke drifted from the kitchen window into the heat of the early August sun that washed over me in a wide bar stretching from the bare patch at the foot of the porch steps to the rutted mud road. Gravel all over the place, but none on the road. Made no sense.

Behind me, the door opened. Hartley said, "How you doin', sweetheart?"

His work boots clumped across the boards of the porch. He plunked his gangly self down, one step up so he could stare down at me. He dragged on his cigarette.

"What do you say, sweetheart? Want a cold beer?"

"No thanks."

"What do you say, sweetheart, we go for a drive to the fire lookout. I'll let you drive."

"No thanks."

I stuck my finger into my glass and stirred the ice cube and, as Hartley got up and stepped past me, I flicked a spray of liquid onto his pant leg. He didn't notice. He clumped across the weed-filled yard and stood beside his Caddy. He'd bought new chrome rims and whitewall tires. He was restoring it, he said, putting on a set of duals, he said. I could tell from the way his lanky frame sagged in his unbuttoned plaid shirt and rumpled work pants that he was drunk. Seven o'clock in the morning.

Baseball hat covering his balding skull, this drunk zombie moron arrived every Friday, spent the weekend, and left Monday morning for his job at the pit. Who knew where he slept through the week. In a zombie crypt with all those other gravel zombies.

"What d'you say, sweetheart? Let's you and me take a drive in my Caddy. We can grab a coffee at Smokey the Bear."

"No thanks."

My mother came out and stood on the top step. "Hartley? Where you goin'?"

Hartley glowered at her.

"What are you doin' out here, Hartley? You said you wanted to play cards. Why didn't you tell me you were comin' out here? I was waitin' for you. I got the cards and—"

"I don't wanna play fucking cards." He lit up a Player's and stood by the gleaming front wheel of his battered Caddy, legs spread like a gunfighter, thumbs hooked in his belt, staring at me.

"Leave Aiyana alone," my mother warned. "Don't get her upset."

"About what?"

"She's upset I won't let her go to Tranta."

"Father Clark said I could go. And it's pronounced Tor-*on*-to."

"Why d'you wanna go to Toro*n*ta?" asked Hartley.

"To try out for Juilliard."

"The Juilliard? That's a strip joint."

I held up the paper where Father Clark had written the address. "Dr. McCoy, Madison Avenue, is not a strip joint. He's going to help me get ready for Juilliard tryouts."

"It's a strip joint. With your looks and body, you'll make a fortune." He took the address from me and brought out a stubby pencil and pad from his shirt pocket.

I tried to grab it back but he blocked me with one shoulder and backed away.

"So me and my buddies can go down and watch the bush bait strip. They got a strip joint in Sudbury called Sights." Hartley stretched his arm out straight and looked down his finger, cocked and pointed. "I got my sights on you, sweetheart."

I snatched back the paper.

"How about I help you practise, give you some free strip lessons?"

"How about you do me a favour and pass out."

Hartley and my mother went inside. They'd be opening the refrigerator, unsnapping a Moosehead, sitting at the table, lighting a Player's. Round and round go the hours, again and again go the days. This was how each rerun day started and this was how each rerun day stopped.

I finished the orange juice. In the kitchen, I rinsed the glass. I picked up Socks, now a heavy lump of old and fat, and took her to my bedroom while I changed into jeans and a t-shirt. Then I gathered the cat up under my arm and sat her on the kitchen table for a moment while I made a purse adjustment. Socks rode around on the purse everywhere I went, but the shoulder strap was too long and it banged on my hip when I walked.

My mother finished her Moosehead and got up. Using the counter for support, she crossed the kitchen and stumbled into the living room. I knew what would happen next. She would collapse into her Sally Ann chair, pick up the remote, turn on a Dr. Phil rerun, and fall asleep.

I listened. Sabrina was in love with James, whom she had given $250,000. But Sabrina had never met James. She didn't know where he lived even. But he looked nice in his picture. Dr. Phil told Sabrina she was stupid for giving her money to a picture.

The saw and wheeze of my mother's snores drowned out Dr. Phil. But I could hear him say clearly: An hour ago, Aiyana, your mother was asleep in her bed. Now, at seven forty in the morning, she's asleep in her chair. That means you're stupider than Sabrina for giving your life to a drunk.

I put the cat on the floor. I turned off the TV and returned to my seat at the kitchen table to study Dr. McCoy's address. One of the numbers was either 6 or 9. There was an O in this line and two Os in this line and an O over here. I remembered how each day from the time I was seven years old, I'd chanted my patterns so my brain didn't go into meltdown: Round and round I go. Round like a circle, round like a plate, round like a satellite dish, that is my fate.

When the grade-one teacher showed me an O drawn on a piece of paper, I told her what it looked like. "A plate."

"Not a plate, Aiyana. Try again."

"A satellite dish." I did not want to say a toilet.

"We've talked about this before, Aiyana. You're mixing up *round* with *around* and *again* with *another*.

"I'm sorry."

"It's a letter of the alphabet, Aiyana. It's used for making words. If I put three together like this…"

The teacher wrote OOO. "How many Os are there?"

"Three."

"What do they look like?"

"Circles?"

"Yes. Good." The teacher put a tail on the O. "What number is that?"

I studied the number. "Nine?"

"Yes, good. You're good with nines."

The teacher pointed to OOO. "Pretend that's a word, Aiyana. What might it be?"

"Same."

"Good, yes, all three are the same. But turn the letters into what could be a word."

"Again?"

The teacher sighed, something she did again and again when she was trying to teach me the alphabet. The teacher started a fresh sheet of paper, as though she thought the paper was to blame. She drew the O. Then she drew a line beside it.

I said, "I think an upside-down balloon on a stick."

"It's a letter b, Aiyana."

I had seen that letter lots of times. But it was not like O, which was always the same. Sometimes it was a letter b and sometimes a letter d and sometimes a 9 and sometimes a 6.

The teacher set the paper aside and wrote CAT in big letters on the board. I studied the white lines on the black and saw TAC. If I looked away and back again, I saw TCA. If I looked longer than a blink, I saw TACCATATCAT. In two blinks I could turn CAT into forty lines of white on the blackboard. But now it didn't matter which of those forty appeared, or that thirty-nine were wrong. Now I knew they all meant the same thing: Socks.

Hartley plodded in from somewhere, a bottle of Canadian Club under his arm. He sailed his hat across the room to the top of the refrigerator. He sat across from me. "Why're you always wearing that feather?"

I touched my hair where the white feather was dangling. "Father Clark gave it to me. It's from the Angel of Mercy. It's a security thing, if you must know."

"Like that stupid cat." He began to shuffle the deck of cards. "I thought the Angel of Mercy was the nurse who killed people."

"That's the other Angel of Mercy. The one who's coming for you, soon I hope."

He dealt himself a hand. "Your mother says your doctor won't sign the forms for your eight-hundred-and-fifty-five-dollar disabled-child allowance because you're not a child anymore. I told her she should ask him to sign the forms for a two-thousand-a-month disabled adult 'cause you're disabled by weirdness." He dealt another hand and picked it up and shuffled and dealt another, slapping the cards onto the table and then gathering them into a reshuffle.

I cradled Socks in the crook of my neck and cuddled her close, waiting for the steady pattern of the little motor.

"Your mother says, 'Get rid of that cat. I hate cats. Why is that cat here instead of at the church where it belongs? And what's that dog doin' around here?'"

"Father Clark died. They boarded up his church."

"When?"

"Friday."

"So give 'em both to Jimmy George."

Hartley threw down the cards and went into the living room. I heard the clatter of plastic as he sorted through his CDs. Then, for the fiftieth time that weekend, Johnny Cash's "Folsom Prison Blues" began, round and round, again and again, drowning out my mother's snores. I hated the sound of those snores. But I also found the steady pattern reassuring.

Hartley returned. He stood in front of me, looking down. "What d'you say, sweetheart? Let's you and me have a little dance."

"What d'you say, Hartley? Let's you and me go to Hollywood so I can put you on Dr. Phil."

I got up to leave. Where I would go, I didn't know, but now that my mother had passed out, I knew what was coming, not a for-sure knowing, but a feeling, if not now, then later in the day, and if not then, then later in the night, and if not then … I chanted my pattern: First This, then That, then This, then That. Round and round I go.

But before I could get away, Hartley's long fingers fastened around my wrist and he wrapped his arm around my waist and, drawing me close, stepped across the room in time with the music until, crossing the centre of the floor, the heel of his work boot caught on the cracked linoleum and he lurched sideways. As he reached for the kitchen counter, I broke free. By the time he'd regained his balance and opened another Moosehead and lit another Player's, I'd scooped up Socks and my purse and the money I'd saved from church cleaning and was out the door.

The weeds grabbed at my sandals as I crossed the yard. I hopped on one foot, then the other, removing the sandals to a barefoot hurry-hurry down the road, glancing back as I went.

He was too drunk to catch me on foot. If he came after me in his Caddy, I could cut across the fields. But he didn't follow me and I reached the church safely. I leaned against Father Clark's car, abandoned now, waiting to be towed away, its gasoline probably siphoned into someone else's. I circled the church, looking for Farley, but he was gone, wandering from trailer to trailer, asking with sad eyes to please take him in. I could take Socks but not Farley. Someone would adopt him. Although, now that the gravel company had bought the land, the trailers sitting on it would soon be gone too.

Now what to do? Yesterday a truck from Sudbury had arrived. I stood by the gate and watched the two men load my piano into the cube van and drive away, bought by some music store in Toronto, they said.

I continued past Harry's to the stop sign at Highway 69. I put on my sandals to cross the asphalt, shimmering in the morning sun. I sat in the ditch next to the one cornfield not yet torn to pieces for gravel. Two cars drove by and then a third. It screeched to a halt. The door swung open and Hartley stepped out.

I jumped up and cut across the ditch and scrambled over the wire fence. I backed into the shoulder-high August corn, Socks pressed against my chest.

He shouted, "Stupid little bush-bait bitch!"

I forced my way farther into the corn. I listened to the mufflers fade away. I pushed through the corn, coming out finally at the rim of a ravine. With my free hand I took off my sandals and waded through the twitch grass into the undergrowth beneath the trees where I sat on a rock, biting the fingernails of my right hand, then my left, going back and forth, following the pattern until I drew blood.

I settled Socks in my lap, my bleeding fingernails tiny red marbles like the ones Socks used to bat across the church basement floor before she got old and fat. I stroked her soft fur. Right away the soothing motor started and I felt better. I'd seen a program on TV about comfort animals. People with mental problems were allowed to take their cats or even a canary into a restaurant so they didn't have a meltdown. I bent my head closer, waiting for the soft, reassuring monotone to soothe away the harsh chords of "Folsom Prison Blues" repeating in my brain the way every piece Chopin wrote echoed in variations through my mind, refusing to let me go until I sat down at the keys of the piano and let my fingers take me with him.

But the piano was gone. No more piano.

Then I remembered Father Clark saying, "There will always be a piano, and where there is a piano there will be a purpose and a plan." He had said this when he showed me Dr. McCoy's letter. "You just don't know yet what the plan is. The church sent me up here to Broken Deer. They figured one winter up here with no purpose or no plan and I'd retire and be collecting my salary from the pension plan instead of from the parish funds."

Then Father Clark's face had lit up and his eyes had twinkled. "Then I met a very little girl with a very big gift, and it was this little girl who gave me the purpose and the plan. So you see, it looks like things just happen at random, but what looks like randomness is really the plan with a little bit of random thrown in to keep you caught up in the purpose. All you have to do is let the purpose take you where the plan wants you to go." He held up his glass of ginger ale. "Here's to the plan."

I climbed barefooted out of the ravine to the edge of the corn. I stood on the roadside. In one direction, trailer park; in the other direction, Juilliard. I refastened the feather, almost ripped off by the cornstalks, and held out my thumb. It was pointing upward, like at the assessment centre. Thumbs up. I watched the approaching car slow to a stop, its signal lights flashing. It was not one of the junkers from the trailer park or one of the gravel zombies from the crypt. I took a deep breath and climbed in.

Too late, I realized I had forgotten Dr. McCoy's letter.

CHAPTER THIRTEEN

Eric

Friday afternoon, I left the office early to start four weeks' vacation, plus two more in lieu of overtime. I had two plans: one, tidy up Julia's estate; and two, get her ashes to the cabin.

Driving up Madison Avenue, I noticed a Reliance Home Comfort truck blocking my spot. I parked in front of 60 Madison, the only derelict house on the otherwise upscale inner-city street, and got out of the restored Wrangler.

A teenage girl stepped toward me, purse hanging from her shoulder, black hair falling forward, partly concealing the cat cradled in her arms. "I'm sorry to bother you. Can you help me?"

She wore no makeup and no jewellery, but there, fastened to one strand of her hair, hung a single white feather. It looked like a perfect match to the one Julia found. She must have noticed me staring at it and read something in my face. Her black eyes shifted from apologetic to guarded.

I asked, "Are you lost?"

"I know the address and I knocked on the door but the woman doesn't know the person I'm looking for so she said telephone the university but when I dial the numbers I can't get through and—"

"Slow down a bit." I put out my hand. "My name is Eric."

"Aiyana," she said. Her grip was firm and her fingers long and slender. Now that I could see her face clearly, I guessed she was around twenty. "What address are you looking for? Which house?"

She nodded in the direction of the yard of weeds bordered by the overgrown hedge of 60 Madison. "It's supposed to be that one, I think."

"Oh … That house is scheduled for demolition."

"People still live there. The woman said it was okay … Are you a university professor?"

I considered my shirt and tie and jacket. "I'm an accountant."

"Oh … I thought…" She glanced at number 60. "I'm not good with numbers. I think this was supposed to be the address but it's not, and when I phone the university it's the wrong number. Could you phone for me?"

"Give me your phone and I—"

"I don't have a phone. But there's one inside. The lady said it was okay."

I followed her up the walk to the front porch, careful not to tread on the rotten bottom step. As we entered the living room, she pointed. "That's Uncle Bill. That's what the lady called him."

Asleep on a couch, hands folded over his bulging belly, face turned to one side, Uncle Bill snored loudly. A line of crumbs trailed across his grey t-shirt to a half-eaten bag of Hostess potato chips on the floor beside a crumpled blanket.

"This is your uncle?" I was confused.

"No. I don't know him. I've never been here before."

But she leaned over and scooped the blanket off the floor. She nudged Uncle Bill's shoulder. He grunted and stirred but didn't wake up. "He's just drunk," Aiyana said flatly. "Passed out." As she covered Uncle Bill with the blanket, gently tucking him in as though she'd known him for years, I noticed her fingers were red from nail-biting. Uncle Bill grunted and muttered something about his couch. The girl leaned back, considering Uncle Bill as though she wanted to help him.

"This is his favourite spot, the lady told me. She was going to give the couch to Goodwill so he'd pass out somewhere else. But they've been evicted. They'll be leaving soon, she said, maybe tomorrow."

I was not liking this, standing uninvited in a drunk stranger's house. "Look, we'll just use my cell. Who should I phone?"

She recited the number. "Ask for the Faculty of Music. Then I'll talk."

I dialled the number. A canned voice said, "Leave a message."

I frowned. "I think that was a private residence."

This time the numbers she gave me were switched, the six for a nine. But the zero was the same. Another canned voice asked me to leave a message.

I felt her eyes on me. She seemed to be wondering about me in the same way she'd been contemplating the uncle. Then abruptly she said, "Socks. Where's Socks?" She hurried down the hall and outside, calling, "Here, Socks! Kitty, kitty, kitty!"

I followed her and stood on the porch. She'd gone partway along the sidewalk, still calling her cat, when she turned in the opposite direction from the Reliance van. She seemed to be listening for something. I came down the porch step to stand beside her.

She glanced at me, her black eyes filled with fear. "I think Hartley's coming. I think I hear his car."

"Who's Hartley?"

She grabbed my arm. "There he is."

A blue Elvis Presley Cadillac screeched to a halt and backed up. A man climbed out and crossed the yard, his work boots slapping through the weeds. He took a pack of Player's from his plaid shirt pocket. "How you doin', buddy? I've come to take the kid home."

She backed up a few steps. "I'm not a kid and I'm not going home."

He lit the cigarette and blew out the match. When he grabbed her hand, she pulled back, stumbled, and fell. But she scrambled up and ran for the house. He caught her from behind and fastened his hand around her upper arm and dragged her to the Caddy. I stepped into his path. When he took a swing at me, Aiyana slammed her elbow into his side and broke free. I grabbed his arm and we stood face to face. His weathered features suggested more years of hard mileage on his lanky body than on his old Caddy.

I let go and backed up, sliding my cell out of my pocket. "I'm calling the police."

A rustle and rattle of metal from behind made me look up. One of the Reliance men, taller than Hartley and twice as heavy, had pushed through the hedge next door. "Back off, slick, or you get the dolly over your head." He hefted the iron frame.

For a moment, Hartley stood his ground. His eyes were cold and fearless, and it seemed even if the Reliance man swung the dolly, Hartley could catch it mid-air. But when the man raised the dolly, Hartley turned, sauntered across the yard, climbed into his Caddy, and drove off, mufflers rumbling.

I thanked the Reliance man, who was watching the car disappear. "An old Coupe Deville. That car would be worth some good money if he fixed it up." He returned to his truck, dragging the dolly behind him.

Aiyana picked up the cat and cuddled it close. Her lips were trembling but she swallowed her tears, willing herself not to cry.

"What was all that about?"

She brushed bits of grass off her legs. "He wants to take me back home."

"Then if you don't want to go you should call the police."

"I'm only seventeen. They'll send me back home whether I want to go or not. Or put me in a shelter. Or phone Family Services." Rubbing her shoulder and arm, she managed a weak smile. "Hartley is my mother's boyfriend. Now you know why I ran away." She flexed the fingers of the hand that had been rubbing her shoulder and arm. "He has a really strong grip. It's a gravel worker thing, where I'm from. Who has the strongest grip." She glanced down the street as though expecting Hartley to return.

"Where are you from?"

"Up north. My mother and I live in a trailer park."

I looked at her more closely. I'd heard the term trailer-park trash plenty of times, but this girl looked decent. Beautiful, in fact. The glistening black hair and the dark eyes and the name, Aiyana, suggested Latina heritage. Especially, the eyes. I'd never seen such deep black eyes.

She stood there, one hand holding the cat, the other rubbing her arm, listening for Hartley, frowning at house number 60.

I needed to help her. "Let me take you to the walk-in clinic for a check over."

"I'll be all right. It's my hands I worry about." She splayed her hands and flexed her fingers. "I don't want him to crush my hands."

"Or I can phone my doctor. Or we go to Emerg. How about the rest of you? Your cheek? It looks a little bruised."

"It's all right."

Gently I pressed on the side of her face with the tips of my fingers. "Does that hurt?"

"No. Really. If he wanted to hurt me, I'd be unconscious. Besides, I don't care, as long as he doesn't crush my hands."

I could not prevent my fingers from lingering on the soft skin of her cheek. I could not stop staring into the depth of her black eyes. I had not looked into any woman's eyes since Julia, and now, I could not help it. I was looking into the eyes of this teenage girl. I couldn't stop myself. And she was looking at me with a wide, unblinking stare as though she could not stop herself.

I stepped back. I shouldn't have touched her, for now she seemed to be wondering about my intentions. Or maybe she was thinking we'd met before. Maybe I knew her from before. But no, a girl this beautiful I would not have forgotten.

As she brushed the hair away from her eyes, the white feather settled for a moment on her shoulder before returning to its place on her chest. I had not paid much attention to Julia's feather, but now, as Aiyana glanced down the street and glanced up at number 60 and then back to me, my eyes fixed on the feather.

"It's an angel feather," she said. "My priest gave it to me." She refastened the feather without disturbing the cat under her arm, nestled on top of the leather purse that was slung over her shoulder.

"Do you have … anything else? A suitcase?"

She shook her head. "Just what I'm wearing. I left in such a hurry I didn't take time to pack."

"You can't go home and get them? Clothes, I mean?"

"I'll never go back home, clothes or no clothes. Besides, it's hours away."

"How about money?"

"I have two hundred dollars, just for spending. Father Clark sent a cheque for living expenses to Dr. McCoy at the university."

"Dr. McCoy? I sometimes get his mail because of the crazy street numbers. But he's at number 90. He's away right now. In Ireland, I think. My neighbour mentioned something about a death in the family."

Her face fell. She looked lost.

I felt lost. I had no idea what to do next. "So now what? Not enough money to live on, no clothes. No Dr. McCoy."

She looked away, hugging the cat, trying to hide her struggle not to cry. "I thought Father Clark had set that up with Dr. McCoy."

"Why not phone Father Clark?"

"He died."

I tried to add this up. I didn't want to get involved, but I couldn't leave her standing on the street. "Here's an idea. I've been renting the apartment above mine for storage. Why don't you stay at least one overnight to get things sorted out?"

She shook her head.

"I understand your concern. As I said, I'm an accountant for the American government. The property is owned by an elderly brother and sister. The vacant apartment has a chain so you can lock yourself in for safety. I have a few things in there that belonged to my girlfriend, Julia. You can use the phone to get things sorted out. Next door used to have a cat so I can probably borrow a litter box."

The girl was staring at me, her face filled with not worry or fear but with something else, more like she was trying to make sense of me.

"We can sort it out tomorrow," I said.

She was cradling the cat, rocking it like a baby.

"If that cat gets away, you might never find it again."

This seemed to convince her. The Reliance van had left so my parking space was clear. I opened the car door and, with the cat cradled in her lap, she settled herself in the front seat. I went around to the driver's side and pulled onto the street.

I could feel her staring at me, it seemed trying to find the words she wanted to say. Finally, she did. "You look familiar. I've been trying to figure it out. I think because a social worker who came when I was little looked something like you."

"What do social workers look like?"

"Older women usually, like I don't know, somebody's mother or like my parish priest, Father Clark. But the social worker I'm thinking about had sandy hair like my dad. Like yours. Sort of. You look like my dad, sort of. Maybe that's it."

I felt her studying me with such a steady, searching stare I was feeling uncomfortable. I had the feeling she already knew all about me. But no, more likely the stare was from fear and suspicion of me. Who knew what horrors she might have come from.

I backed into my parking spot and shut off the Wrangler. She slipped the purse over her shoulder, massaged her wrist, flexed the fingers of the injured hand, and cradled up the cat, which seemed able to adjust to any position, under one arm, upside down, whatever.

"That's a pretty good-natured cat," I said. "Unlike that Hartley character."

She nodded as she unbuckled and opened the door.

She followed me up the front walk, the snap of her sandals sounding so much like an echo from Julia's sandals that I turned to look back. The lush lawn, divided into two perfectly manicured squares with flower beds bordering each property line, was the same, and the sound of the sandals was the same. But it had been something about the person wearing them that made me look back to see if she was Julia.

I held the front door for her to go inside.

On the mat she bent over to adjust her sandals. "This strap is broken so they walk kind of wonky."

Julia had about ten pairs of sandals. I decided to offer Aiyana one before she left. We walked down the hall to the stairs. I noted she was six inches shorter than me, about as tall as Julia. I led the way up the stairs and along the second-floor hallway to the vacant apartment. "Sorry, no AC in this hot weather. The wiring is too old to handle anything more than a fan."

Aiyana surveyed the room, frowning. She looked confused, like she couldn't make out what she was seeing. I flipped the switch for the overhead light.

"Where is Julia?" Aiyana asked.

I was startled. I didn't remember mentioning Julia's name. But I must have.

"Dead."

"Dead? She died here?"

"A car accident two months ago returning from her cabin. May twenty-fourth. I came into a curve too fast and rolled the Wrangler. Since then, I've been, you know…" For some reason, I had the urge to tell her about my feelings, how I'd been blaming myself.

I was about to make a confession, when she asked, "Where did it happen?"

"Near Sudbury." Then I added, "The day before it happened, she found a white feather, like yours. The angel left it for her, she said."

Aiyana drew a sharp breath. She turned around to look, and I turned around to look, expecting to see the angel that must have nudged her from behind.

"Julia believed it was a good sign if a feather was left in your path."

Aiyana faced me, her eyes questioning. She seemed to be having trouble understanding the feather connection. She said, "It's the Angel of Mercy that leaves the feather. Are you sure Julia died?"

"Of course. We had a funeral, did all the, you know, stuff."

The answer seemed to make sense to her. She continued to investigate the room, looking in drawers, examining each item of furniture, running the red tips of her unusually long nail-bitten fingers along the top of the dresser. But it wasn't like snooping. It was more like recognizing, the way you would if you'd just come home from being gone a long time. Then, noticing a box of classical records, she knelt to look through them.

"They're all old LPs," I explained. "Mostly Chopin. They're from her grandmother, along with the old record player. When I get everything sorted out, I'll give them away."

"Did Julia play these? I've never seen them on vinyl." Her eyes were wide as she sorted through them, marvelling at each in turn. "I recognize the covers from books Father Clark showed me: Hungarian Rhapsody, Revolutionary Etude. Did she play them?"

"She might have. I'm not the best judge of music. I'm tone-deaf."

"Tone-deaf?"

Her unblinking stare made me explain. "I can't hear the different notes."

"But you can hear other stuff, different noises?"

"I'm not deaf like noise deaf. It's just the different notes I can't hear."

"Oh, hmm. I've never heard of that." She turned back to the cover picture of Chopin. "I played these on the piano when I was little. I could play every piece that Chopin wrote but I couldn't match my socks. Too many colours."

"Too many colours?"

"There's something wrong with my brain. Like a dog smells a hundred times more smells than people, I hear a hundred times more notes and see a hundred times more colours and feel a hundred times more feelings and … who knows what else is the matter with me."

She continued to sort through the LPs. "I didn't know the names of the pieces of music. Father Clark had to go to the music store to find out what I was playing."

The priest again. "Well, I'd be no help. To me, everything sounds like Melody in Plunky Flat."

She set the LPs aside to adjust her sandal, no doubt damaged in her scuffle with Hartley. I wanted to suggest that she could go through all Julia's sandals and, for that matter, Julia's clothes and take whatever fit. I could lay her entire wardrobe on the bed and she could take what she wanted. But then I remembered she had no place to live. And then I thought, why am I doing this? This girl is a complete stranger.

She sat on the edge of Julia's chesterfield and began to fix her hair. First she removed the feather and placed it beside her. Then she took a hairbrush from her purse, leaned her head to one side, and began to brush with quick, practised strokes. Then she did the other side, electricity snapping with each sweep of the brush. Finished, she refastened the feather. She splayed her hands and studied the chewed nails. She flexed her wrist and bent back each finger. Then she settled onto Julia's chesterfield and wrapped one long leg around the other.

Julia also had long legs and would sit with one wrapped around the other in that same spot on that same chesterfield. Julia liked to say, "I'll put a bug in his ear." Watching Aiyana, I had this feeling now, that Julia had put a bug in my ear about this girl, giving me a hint about something, although I didn't know what. But I sensed something was going on between me and Aiyana and Julia that I couldn't put my finger on.

I needed to clear my head, like get a breath of fresh air. So that when my cellphone rang reminding me of my appointment with my lawyer at five o'clock, I didn't have any trouble saying to Aiyana, "While I'm gone you can rearrange the furniture however you want. I won't be long."

She said, "Thank you."

CHAPTER FOURTEEN

Eric

After the meeting with the lawyer to discuss Julia's estate, I stopped at the supermarket and bought pork chops, mushroom soup, potatoes, carrots, and bread, enough for a decent meal. I didn't know why I decided on pork chops and mushroom soup — yes, I did. In the cabin, I'd noticed a recipe pinned to the cupboard door, Julia's cabin recipe: Pork Chop and Mushroom Soup. Simple enough that even I could do it.

I wasn't feeling right about having dinner with this girl, who was right now maybe lying on Julia's bed. It didn't seem appropriate. But, I reasoned, having dinner wasn't like going out for dinner. It was giving her something to eat. And she probably wasn't lying on Julia's bed.

Then another thought troubled me. The return of that lunatic with the Caddy. By the time I parked in front of the Wilson house, I wasn't thinking about dinner. I was thinking about Aiyana lying dead on the floor. I hurried up the walk and along the hall and checked both apartments. She wasn't there. There were no signs of any scuffle. I couldn't find the cat. She must have gone to the university, got her business sorted out, and was on her way elsewhere. I felt relieved at not needing to look after some girl I'd found on the street.

But back in my kitchen, partway through my second cup of coffee, I heard the snap of her sandals at the outer door. They continued along the hall and up the stairs to Hilda's apartment and then, after a few minutes, down to mine.

She seemed more relaxed as she came in and sat at the kitchen table. "I borrowed a litter box from next door and fixed up a blanket for Socks to sleep on."

"You must be hungry." I began to unwrap the pork chops. "Let's see what I can put together."

"I'll help you." But when she tried to pick up the frying pan she flinched.

"I can do it." I took it from her.

She picked up the can opener for the mushroom soup, but again, she flinched from the pain.

"I can do this. You need to rest that wrist."

While the chops simmered and the mushroom soup murmured, I sat on the chesterfield with a cup of coffee. Aiyana sat in Julia's recliner. She'd poured herself a glass of orange juice, which she placed on the coffee table, which was also Julia's. I got up and brought a coaster from the kitchen for her glass. I caught her giving me that look, staring at me with a combination of curiosity and fear.

"Anything else I can get you?"

"No thank you."

This time of day, I usually read the New York Times, seated in Julia's recliner where the light was better, now taken over by this girl who had picked up the photo album of Julia from the coffee table. She was concentrating so hard on each picture, I thought she was having difficulty making out the details. I got up to turn on the lamp next to her elbow.

"This is Julia?"

"On a canoe trip."

After she examined all the pictures, she glanced at Julia's framed Ryerson grad photo, formerly in her bedroom, now hanging on the wall directly across from the recliner. Aiyana got up to look at the picture more closely. "She's wearing a cross. Was she Catholic?"

I hadn't noticed the thin gold necklace with a tiny cross. "Well …
yes she was."

She looked over at the piano. "Are you going to keep the ashes
there?" She said this as though she thought on the piano was not the
right place.

"Her grandmother wants me to spread the ashes at the lake. I've
never been involved in this sort of thing so I'm feeling a bit lost.
Disperse her ashes, if that's the word. But the only way there is by
canoe, and I'm not much good with a canoe."

Aiyana turned away and carried her drink into the bathroom. I
could see her in the mirror fixing her hair again, and there she was
doing it again, refastening the feather. When she finished, she came
back, picked up the cat, and sat in the recliner. She placed her glass
on the coaster and curled her bare feet underneath her. She picked up
her purse from beside the chair, opened it, and pulled out a silver
lighter with a red top and a picture of a red cap on the front.

"I grabbed this when I left home — my father's Red Cap lighter."

She raised the top and flicked the wheel. The flint sparked and a
blue flame appeared. I waited for her to take out cigarettes, knowing
I would have to tell her she couldn't smoke inside. That was a Wilson
rule. But she snapped down the lid and closed her fingers over it as
though she didn't want to see that flame again.

"What are you going to do with all this furniture?" she asked.

"Sell it, give it away. But first, the will has to be settled."

"A car accident." She looked puzzled. "And the day before the
accident she found a white feather."

She seemed to be turning this feather over and over in her mind
as she opened her hand and stared at the lighter. With the fingers of
the uninjured hand, she turned the lighter over twice before gripping
it right side up. She spun the wheel and the blue flame leaped up on
the wick.

She studied the wavering fire. "You were with her."

"Yes."

"Couldn't you save her?"

"Internal injuries. No."

"Where near Sudbury did it happen?"

"Sideroad 15."

She snapped down the lid and then sparked the lighter again. She did this several times, studying the flame the same way she'd studied Julia's grad photo.

"Um … why are you—"

"I like to look at each new flame. I see different colours in each one every time I light it."

She flicked it open again. Apparently she didn't like what she was seeing this time, because she immediately blew the flame out and put the lighter back into her purse and said, "When I was little, my father fell through a hole in the ice and drowned at three o'clock in the afternoon. This lighter was in his pocket."

"I'm so sorry." I meant it.

"After the funeral, I started doing this. I was only six but I already had strong fingers. So I would light his lighter so I could warm his hands."

"You wanted his hands to be warm? Is that some sort of tradition?" I was thinking that maybe in her family background it was like spreading the ashes.

"Not really. When I found him in the ice on the shoreline he wasn't wearing the mitts I'd got him for Christmas. What happened was, the day after Christmas, my father and grandfather and I went ice fishing off Devil's Island. You cut a hole in the ice and sit in the sun on a winter's day and fish. I was lying on my back in the snow, making snow angels."

At the mention of angels she paused. The look she gave the urn sent shivers of cold fingers up the back of my neck.

"For some reason, my grandfather went back to the snowmobile we'd driven across the ice. My hands were a little cold so my father had taken off my mitts, which were the same as his mitts. He lit this lighter to warm them up, my hands that is. He put my mitts back on me and stood up, and waved down at me. I was half-buried in the snow, peeking up through the white flakes at his face in the middle of the sky. It was blue, with different blues moving around. On a sunny day, I can see all the different blues moving around like in a kaleidoscope. But I wasn't seeing any blues on either side of his face. I was only seeing his face, and he was only seeing me. He stepped back, smiling and waving — and then he fell into the hole and disappeared under the ice."

Her eyes became distant. "The cold water stops your heart in five minutes. My grandfather heard the splash and came running back. 'How long ago did he go in?' he asked. I didn't know. He asked again. 'One minute? Five minutes?' I didn't know. I was only six. My grandfather is bigger and stronger than everyone. If it was less than five minutes, he'd have gone in after him. But I didn't know. I had to decide but couldn't. I had to make a choice I couldn't make."

"But you were only six."

"I know. I was only six."

She was seated across from me. I tried to meet her eyes, but she looked away. Then she said, "When I found my father in the shoreline ice the next spring, he had the lighter in his pocket. See the red hat? I stood the hat right side up on the kitchen table and let it dry out. When I flipped open the top, the wick caught right away on the first try. How could that lighter have been under water all that time and still work? I've never had to fill it. It's like, as long as I keep lighting it, it'll never run out of fluid and I'll be able to warm his hands whenever he asks me."

I imagined her as a child, in tears, kneeling at the side of her drowned father, a much different picture than the ones of seven-year-old Julia holding a string of fish, smiling into the camera. I remembered the cold fingers creeping up my back as I knelt next to Julia in the roadside ditch, listening to those whispered words, *Where are you?* I wanted to tell Aiyana about those cold fingers. I wanted to say, Maybe you can lend me that lighter so I can warm Julia's cold hands. More than anything, I wanted to say, How does your father ask you to warm his hands? Tell me how to do that so I can ask Julia:

Please let me warm your cold hands. But the thought of going there, wherever there was, gave me a scary feeling, like when I was five and the thought of a bogeyman in my closet made me afraid to go there.

She picked up the cat, which was curled up in her lap, and cuddled it under her chin.

I returned to the kitchen to finish cooking dinner. I glanced through the door to the living room. Aiyana was standing by the piano, staring at the urn. With her right arm partly raised, she seemed to want to touch it but could not, wanting to but afraid to, both at the same time. So instead, she sat on the bench. She ran the tips of the fingers of her left hand along the ebony keys and leaned over to examine a small chip on one black key. Then she got up and came back to the kitchen and stood next to me. She spread the long fingers of each hand on the counter. "When I was eight, I played for a school play, offstage so no one could see me. I was there but not there, part of the play but not really. That's how I'm feeling now. Here but not here."

This bizarre adventure was getting spooky. "Well, you've just run away, feeling alone … and lost."

"Standing at the piano with that urn on top, I get a feeling from the urn, it feels like, I don't know … and when I look at Julia's picture hanging on the wall, it seems like … I don't know, like she's in the frame but she's also outside the frame."

I nodded. "I think … I don't know … but I think … urns do that to people."

"I don't mean that. You're looking at what's in the frame but I'm seeing what's happening outside the frame."

I didn't know what that meant but this didn't matter. She was looking so fragile, I needed to say something more. "You just told me about making a choice, your father or your grandfather. But if you were only six years old, you would've felt like you were standing off to one side, not in the frame, not knowing what you were being asked to know. So maybe standing off, you know, standing by Julia's picture … and my God … you were only six years old."

She sat at the kitchen table. "I can hear the mushroom soup gurgling in that pan."

"Oh, you're right. It's probably finished."

"I don't mean it's finished. I mean what I'm hearing — you're going to find this silly — what I'm hearing in that mushroom soup, when I found my father dead in the shoreline ice, the water he was lying in was gurgling and he was the same colour as mushroom soup."

"My God. And you were six years old."

She picked up the cat as it wandered past. "But something else, something strange, I seemed to know which one to pick, like having the answer but afraid it's the wrong answer. It was an accidental drowning so they did an autopsy. My dad had pancreatic cancer when he died."

"In other words..." I tried to phrase this delicately. "With cancer ... I mean ... so you accidentally made the right choice."

"It wasn't accidental. I had the feeling, like intuition, as though I knew which one to choose. I knew."

I wanted to say, A lucky guess. There could be no other answer.

She settled the cat in her lap. She opened her purse and brought out her wallet. "I have some pictures."

My God. Pictures of the body of her drowned father? But I couldn't help myself. I sat beside her to look. But no. The first was Aiyana in front of some kind of tower dressed in shorts and t-shirt. With her long black hair fallen across her chest and her skin brown against the treed background, the picture would have made a good suntan-lotion advertisement.

She said, "That's taken at the fire lookout. In the summer there's always a forest ranger up there watching for fires."

She showed me another. She was sitting on the hood of the Caddy, arms wrapped around one bare leg, which was drawn up with one bare foot resting on the fender, her head turned, looking at something to the right of the camera. The way her hair hung forward hiding her face reminded me of Julia. Except that Julia had short hair. Maybe the way that one bare leg was drawn up reminded me of Julia.

Still not answering, she brought out a third picture, rowboats tied to a dock. "That's Jimmy George's skiff. When he gets drunk, he climbs in there to sleep it off. Across the lake is a deep part. There were always stray cats hanging around. If he caught one, he'd take it fishing. He'd row over there and throw it as far as he could, into the water. He said he was going to take Socks fishing, but my grandfather said, 'If you take Socks fishing, I'll take you fishing.'"

She cradled the cat under her chin. "Socks was my security thing. Still is, I guess. One time, Jimmy and Hartley caught two tomcats that were going around bothering everyone with their yowling. While Hartley held them, Jimmy tied their tails together and then threw them in. They would have drowned for sure but they started fighting and the string broke."

"My God! Why didn't anyone phone the Humane Society?"

She rolled her eyes. "In the Broken Deer Double-Wides Trailer Park? I wish."

I remembered. "Broken Deer is near the Lost Loon Lakes."

"Yes, I know. That's where I'm from. I know all the lakes from fishing with Grandpa Willie."

She reached down to take off her sandals. The straps across the toe were close-woven so that her toes weren't visible. Julia had a black pair like that. When she took them off, she'd say, "Hello. Hello, toes. Time for a breath of fresh air." For just a second I hesitated, waiting to hear those exact words. And because I hesitated, in that second, I thought I heard not *Where are you?* but *Where is she from?*

I checked the pork chops. She stood beside me, looking down. "I'm sorry. I don't think I can eat those bits of mushroom."

"In the soup? Do you want me to pick them out?"

"No thank you. I'm not hungry."

"Can I make you something else?" I was relieved when she said no. I had nothing else. Besides, her mention of the mushroom soup reminded me that the recipe said to simmer for five minutes. The pork chops were probably tough as leather by now.

While I ate, she looked through the bookshelf. There were no books for teenagers, no easy-read novels of any sort that I could offer her. But lots of accounting texts. I kept them like other people kept those leather-bound classics that never got removed from the top shelf. Aiyana stared for a while at my swimming trophies and at the picture of my Harvard swimming team. I wanted to say, I'm the one with the red bathing suit.

From the bottom shelf, she selected one of Julia's Outdoor Canada magazines. She sat on the piano bench, the injured hand resting in the lap of her jeans, and leafed through.

"There's an article Julia wrote in there," I said. "The crow is the smartest of all birds. They have their own language."

"My grandfather knows all about nature. He's a hunting-and-fishing guide."

Maybe now was the time to sort out this girl's background and figure out a way to get her back home. "I don't mean to pry, but what was this meeting with Dr. McCoy about?"

"To take piano lessons."

"You ran away from home to take piano lessons?"

"Sort of, yeah."

She set the magazine aside and swung her legs over the bench. With the uninjured hand, she ran the keys. "It's in tune," she said. "But this chip should be fixed so the damp doesn't get under the finish."

When she leaned forward to examine the chipped key, my eyes were drawn to the grass stain on the back of her t-shirt. Maybe now was the time to offer her that black sweater Julia wore with her jeans, which were identical to this girl's jeans.

"Aiyana, I want to help out. No clothes, running away from home, this Hartley character, all of it not sounding very happy. How can I help?"

She stared at the keys, as though in their black-and-white pattern she might find an answer to my question. Finally, she said, "When I got into your Wrangler and we drove away from that house with that drunk uncle, I thought at last everything was going to be all right. I'm safe now. It wasn't a thought. It was a feeling that turned into a thought. I don't know why I felt that or thought that, because as soon as I got here, I started feeling, this isn't right. At first, I thought it was all the furniture. But then, when you told me about the ashes, I started feeling something else. The best explanation I can make is, the minute I walked in the door I felt like a stray cat coming into a house and realizing there's already a cat living there."

She got up and went into the bathroom. To brush her hair again, I thought. Fix her feather again. The water began running into the sink. When it stopped, a muffled sob floated through the door. After a few minutes, she came out and announced, "I have to tell you something. Standing at the piano, with that urn on top, I get a feeling, I don't know, like I'm inhaling someone else's air, or maybe like the thoughts of someone else are pushing their way into my thoughts, or I don't know, like the emotions of someone else are pushing their way into my emotions. Like in a transplant, when you get someone else's heart."

She turned and went upstairs to Hilda's apartment. I heard the door close and the lock rattle into place. I settled myself into Julia's recliner.

Aiyana. She looked Middle Eastern or maybe Brazilian. And her hands? Not the nails she'd bitten almost bloody from worry, but the long fingers. And her eyes, like searchlights, like she was seeing things the rest of us couldn't see. There was something about her, like looking through fog, like knowing something's there, but you can't get to it. You can't put your finger on it.

As I was getting ready for bed, a gentle tap-tap came from the door. Aiyana looked bashful as she stepped inside.

"Can't sleep?" I asked.

She shook her head.

I nodded toward the chesterfield and we both sat, she with head bowed, left hand to her mouth, teeth-bitten nails chewed bloody. The cat came from somewhere and settled in her lap.

She said, "There's something we need to do, you and me, to make it right. You said you wanted to take the ashes to Julia's cabin, but you weren't good with a canoe. I think it would be a good idea if we did that, like, rent a sixteen-foot fibreglass, at least sixteen feet, no smaller. I'll go with you. I think we should do that. I know we should do that — the filmy shadow I see floating like black lace above the urn, you have to put her back in her urn and you have to put her back in her frame."

I thought, no thank you. This is becoming too weird. The ashes could wait. But then I thought, if the cabin was near where she lived, I could investigate her home situation, check out the mother, look into what was going on with this priest, find out more about the grandfather, go to the nearest police station to find out what could be done about Hartley. Then leave her there. This was too freaky. This was the Twilight Zone.

"Good idea," I said. "Thank you. We'll figure everything out tomorrow. And right now I'll make up the bed in Hilda's. I can set out a pair of Julia's pyjamas for you … just … well…"

I glanced at her, suddenly wondering, Why am I giving Julia's pyjamas to this stranger? Her eyes held mine for a moment. They seemed to be saying, Why are you giving me Julia's pyjamas? But her voice seemed relaxed when she said, "I'm used to wearing second-hand clothes. Almost everything I wore was second-hand. Where I'm from clothes are clothes. So yeah, I guess. In fact, for me to do the same thing I've always done, like wearing other people's clothes, is like following the pattern." She shrugged. "It's weird, I know, but I like patterns." She went to the door of my apartment. I watched her go along the hall to the stairway leading to the upper floor. Her image, framed in the hallway silhouette — the fingers of one hand to her mouth, the fingers of the other hand holding that feather — sent conflicting tingles of cold shivers up the nape of my neck, making me glance back, I don't know at what. I couldn't put my finger on it.

CHAPTER FIFTEEN

Eric

Aiyana arrived at my door right on time at 5:00 a.m. wearing Julia's Wolf Society top and Julia's jean cut-offs, all set and ready to go. I finished packing my camping supplies, which amounted to hot dogs and matches for a fire plus a knife and binoculars I'd bought from the outfitters. The urn was sealed in a cardboard box. One problem remained. If I brought the cat, Aiyana would know I might not be bringing her back. Well, I might have inherited a cat. Better than inheriting both cat and girl.

We drove four hours to the Highway 69 cut-off, Aiyana biting her nails the whole way. I'd intended to buy her some sort of equipment at the drug store to stop her nail-biting but I hadn't found the time. It was a quiet drive, Aiyana saying nothing, staring out the window. By noon, we'd reached a sideroad that continued through a desolate stretch of bush and opened onto the village of Broken Deer. Aiyana pointed to the boarded-up church. "No more Father Clark." She pointed to the two-storey clapboard store advertising Cheap Cigarettes. "There's Harry's." She pointed to the sign for Broken Deer Double-Wides. "There's where I used to live. Near the back by the water."

The mishmash of double-wides on cement blocks scattered among deserted lots looked no different from what Floridians call the Canada-goose summer slipstream, half-empty trailer parks one after the other, stretching from Jacksonville to Miami. As Broken Deer faded away in my rear-view mirror, I saw on either side fields of both exhausted and working gravel pits. We passed a sign for Gravel Works, one of the accounts I was working on. I was startled. "This is a subsidiary of Luck Stone Corp."

"What's that?"

"An American aggregate company."

For the first time, I saw gravel as something besides a number on a balance sheet. Formerly, the word sand would bring up thoughts of a seaside beach, and lumber would trigger visions of growing trees. But gravel had no more meaning for me than the word mud. Until this minute. From now on, gravel would represent desolation.

From the moment we'd entered the Broken Deer Lakes region, Aiyana had faded into a dejected slouch. Her face partly hidden by her hair, she stared down at the scabbed fingers in her lap. I didn't need to see her face to know she was disturbed at being back home.

I said, "A nice sunny day. The trip across the lake will be easy."

No response. We continued along a potholed gravel road and turned in the direction of Crow Rapids, thirty kilometres. We arrived at the Little Lost Loon Lake sign, a hand-painted board on a hydro post. We followed the two-rut road to the water. She pointed where to park the Jeep. She got out and began to unfasten the canoe.

"Let me do it," I said. "You have to release these tie-downs and then slide it off."

She stepped back and stood by the rear door, scowling at me as I struggled to solve the impossible knots that the trip had fastened into the ties. After a few minutes of fumbling, the canoe was free. Then without my help, despite her injured hand, she slipped the canoe onto her shoulders and carried it along the path, through the brush to the water's edge where she flipped it and set it down. She kicked off her sandals and waded in, pulling the canoe with her. Then, in one swift motion no more complicated than sitting in a chair, she climbed in and settled on her haunches in the bow, no life jacket, although the rental had supplied two. I set our gear between the seats and fastened my life jacket. I placed the cardboard box containing the urn under my seat and managed a tippy boarding.

We set off.

Now that I was on the water, I resented her presence on this beautiful August morning with its clear blue sky. I had the feeling Julia was with me, seated in the bow in her Wolf Society top, shoulders back, paddling with strong, even strokes. I didn't want to be babysitting this seventeen-year-old runaway with a feather in her hair, probably a pigeon's.

Stop it. Aiyana was decent. And polite, with pleases and thank-yous, appreciative of what I was doing for her. Besides, today she was helping me.

I was burned out from the emotions of the last few months. I preferred the world of mathematics, the exact truth of numbers, no uncertainty, no illusions, and no guilt. Guilt was what this trip was about, highlighted by this girl, who'd been spinning a web of psychic nonsense about a lighter that should not light and a dead father in the mushroom soup and the ghost of Julia living in the urn.

I would watch the wind on the surface of the water turn that part of Julia that was mineral back into mineral and that part of her that was water back into water and that part of her that was energy back into nothing. This thought stopped me midstroke. Julia had written an article on the idea, that energy does not go back into nothing. Energy changes forms but energy does not go into nothing, because energy never dies.

More psychic nonsense.

Yet, in another way, I was glad she was with me, wearing that pair of Julia's jean shorts, which had shrunk too small for her, kneeling like Julia in that same position in the front of the canoe, so much like Julia that she could have been her. Especially with that feather. Or maybe it was because of the feather that my mind was flipping from Julia to Aiyana, creating the ominous image of both seated in front of me.

And there was something ominous about this lake, on all sides bush thick as a jungle, full of every kind of biting bug imaginable — deer flies, horseflies, dragonflies, crocodile flies — worse than the Everglades. At least in the Everglades, the water below the canoe was not forty feet of melted ice that would freeze you to death in five minutes.

Ominous. The stillness of the flat blue water, no wind, sound, or movement other than the slap of the paddles underlining the silence between us, reminding me of the empty silence of the apartment waiting for me as soon as I had put both Aiyana and Julia to rest.

Time for a break. Somewhere within the walls of trees and steep-faced cliffs, I needed to find a place to stop and uncramp my legs. I angled toward an open space of shoreline, the same place as the last time, this time with no ducks. Aiyana grabbed a stunted bush growing in a crack in the flat rock at the water's edge.

"Not too close," I said. "I don't want to scrape the side."

We got out and hauled the canoe onto the shore.

I said, "This is a good place for an early lunch. We can build a fire and roast the hot dogs."

"The fire lookout isn't far from here. We're in extreme high hazard. If they see your smoke, they won't like it."

I gathered up some sticks and broke them and laid out the paper I'd packed in a separate plastic bag. This time I wanted my fire to work.

"I think maybe it's too dry for a fire," she said. "If the lookout sees the smoke he'll have to check it out. We should wait until we get to the cabin."

"The day Julia and I canoed to the cabin we were going to roast hot dogs here. But didn't. I want to do it now."

From the pocket of my plaid Woodsman shirt, I took my waterproof matches and lit my paper, which lit the smaller sticks, which snapped and crackled in the larger sticks.

"You don't cook on the fire," she said. "You cook on the coals."

"I cook hot dogs over an open fire."

I tried to pay no attention to her frown as I opened my cooler and took out the wieners wrapped in tin foil and the buns in Saran wrap and the two containers of relish and mustard. I tried not to pay any attention to her scowls as I took out the hunting knife that was strapped to my belt. I found two sticks and trimmed each to a point.

She said, "The sticks should be green. Or they'll burn."

Green sticks. Okay. I set my knife down and went looking for two green sticks. When I returned a moment later, she was balancing my knife across two fingers. Then, holding it by the blade tip, she drew it back and swung overhand. The knife arced through the air, turned end over end twice, and thwunked into the trunk of a nearby birch. She pulled it out and walked back for another throw, this time from farther away. Again the knife arced twice and bull's-eyed the same spot.

"Aiyana, that's a new knife. A very expensive one, I might add."

She took one of the sticks I'd gathered, sharpened the end, and gave it to me. "My weapon of choice, a hunting knife. It got me good tips."

"Good tips? From doing what?" I slid a wiener onto my stick and squatted next to the fire.

"Willie — my grandfather — taught me. I would gut fish for the American tourists. When I was done, I'd do the knife show for tips."

I didn't want to get into the ice-fishing accident, if that was why she'd brought the topic up. We were both quiet for a while, our hot dogs sweating over the flames, until she said, "Willie knows all about the woods and the lakes and the rivers and trees and knives. And green sticks. Taught to him by his grandfather, I guess."

I was feeling defensive and I didn't want her to have the last word. "Maybe by Grey Owl."

"Who?"

"My dad is British. He told me Grey Owl was a distant relative."

She was staring at her wiener sizzling in the flames. She seemed to be giving Grey Owl some thought before she said, "Never heard of him."

I wrapped my burned wiener into a bun and handed the package to her.

"Your J stroke is all wrong," she said. "Too much drag."

I settled on a rock with my hot dog.

"You paddle like you're hoeing the garden." She was nibbling on her hot dog, staring across the water.

I said, "I guess your grandfather lives around here."

"He's away now. He's guiding an extreme-adventure trip near James Bay."

"Oh. Wow. James Bay. But what's an extreme-adventure trip?"

"CEOs from New York City dress up in jeans and plaid shirts and hunting knives and hire Willie to guide them into the wilderness lakes. They take pictures of one another holding up the fish, splake usually, and then they leave the fish I gutted to rot in the boat and fly home and show their pictures around the office."

I noted the scorn but let it go. "And what does your mother do?"

Her eyes filled with tears and she looked off, trying to blink them away. For some reason, I'd hit a nerve. But whatever it was, I didn't want to get into that either, whatever it might be. I took out another wiener and stuck it on my stick. After a few minutes, she said, "She's the prime minister of Canada."

I was sitting and she was standing, looking down at me; yesterday she was homeless and helpless and dejected, but today she was full of anger, directed at me.

"I don't understand why you're attacking me."

"Because you tricked me. You're taking me home."

"I'm not taking you home."

"I'm bush bait picked up off the street. I'm not what you want so now you're taking me back to the bush."

I shaded my eyes so I could look directly up at her and read her answer to my lie. "I'm not taking you home. We're here because I need your help with the canoe. That's why we're here."

She sat on the rock and nibbled at the hot dog. I waited for what would come next. Finally, she said, "When I was little, the kids used to trick me. I got good at reading the signs. I know when I'm being tricked."

"Oh, yeah, kids can be cruel. So … how did they trick you?" I was thankful for the reprieve: Now that she was onto me, I had to get her talking about her home life in advance, so that I could help her sort through the mother, the priest, the boyfriend, get it all sorted out, and then say, Since we're so close to where you live, how about I take you home so you can get a new start, a new beginning? Something like that.

"They tricked me by lying to me. They'd say, 'Aiyana. Millie is waiting for you behind the ice hut.' And then when I got there it would be Bucky Beaver and six buddies. At first, Father Clark taught me to turn the other cheek. But as I got older, I didn't want to turn the other cheek anymore."

"Well, you became a teenager. Teenagers sharpen their teeth on the bones of their parents, teachers, authority figures." I liked the tone of "authority figures." It helped reduce the bite of her attempts to humiliate me. Especially since, in fact, in this situation, I was the authority figure, now needing to sort out a situation that required some outside authority, a job I'd not asked for, by the way, picked up off the street, by the way.

"They teased me because I couldn't match socks."

"Why couldn't you?"

"I told you. I have trouble with colours."

I turned my wiener and held it higher. "So you're colour-blind like I'm tone-deaf. Julia loved the colours up here. She loved the blues and greens of the trees and the water, loved getting out of the city and back to nature."

My wiener sizzling, I slipped it into the bun. "I came up with her just that one time, the weekend she got killed. I thought it would be a good place to propose. I can't imagine being colour-blind. Missing all this."

"I'm not colour-blind. I have synesthesia. That's what the kids teased me about. I see too many colours."

Synesthesia. I wanted to say, What's that, another weird ritual, like lighting a lighter?

She said, "You've never heard of synesthesia, I know. I see more colours than other people. Sometimes I can see coloured energy in other people."

I understood that one because of Julia's article. "Julia was into that, about coloured energy. She said some people can see it around each person. She said we're all broadcasting our energy field without knowing it." I felt pleased with myself; we were having a conversation. "Julia said your aura is there when you're born. Everyone has one."

"What colour was Julia's aura?"

"She didn't tell me, and I couldn't see it. I don't have the gift like she did. She wrote all kinds of articles on extrasensory perception, weird psychic stuff. It's sort of religious gone bendy. I don't believe any of it. Hamburger Helper, I call it. Holy water, what is that? Water is water."

"Not really." Her eyes swept the surface of the lake. "There are different kinds of water, the same as there are different kinds of snow." Then she added, "The same as there are different kinds of people with different auras, like my mother and my grandfather, if that's who you're trying to find out about, both people but with so different energy. If you were tricking me into going back to my Grandpa Willie, I might think about it. But he's not here. If you're thinking about taking me back to my mother, I won't go."

Now, although I didn't really want to go there, now seemed like a good time to try again. "Tell me about your mother."

"What about her?"

"What does she do?"

"What do you mean?"

"I mean, you like music. Is she a music teacher?"

"Is she a music teacher? No, she's an accountant."

"You're kidding."

"Yes, I am kidding."

"So what does she do?"

"She's the mayor of Broken Deer. She has her own airplane to fly back and forth to New York."

"Aiyana, stop it. I'm trying to have a conversation about you and your mother."

"You said I wasn't an adult."

"I did not say that. When did I say that?"

"You said I'm a teenager sharpening my teeth on authority figures. If you want to see how sharp they can be, keep asking me about my mother."

She fell silent. Then she said, "I shouldn't have said that. But this lake is bringing back memories of the trailer park and memories of my father. I can hear him, sighing sort of. And now Julia, in that cardboard box. I can hear her, sighing sort of."

"Hear her sighing? Like whispering?"

"It's like flowing. It's like echoes from across the water I shouldn't be hearing because I'm out of earshot."

Flowing, from the box at my feet, echoes from across the water, father in the mushroom soup. "I'm sorry I got you into this, Aiyana. This trip is hard for me so it must be hard for you too. I understand."

"I'm not too sure you can understand."

"Then, please, explain it."

She became thoughtful, her black eyes staring off. She lifted a strand of hair and studied the feather. "My mother is not the mayor or the prime minister and she doesn't drive her own airplane. She collects welfare and she drinks. That's what she does. And smokes cheap cigarettes. That's what we do in Broken Deer. Collect welfare and smoke cigarettes and drink, and I don't mean orange juice and coffee. We don't have little coasters to put our glasses on. We don't have coffee tables. Every month the government sends us our welfare cheques, and instead of buying coffee tables and little coasters to put our orange-juice glasses on, we sit in our double-wides and drink straight out of our whisky bottles because all the glasses are dirty and we don't have dishwashers to put them in to get them clean for the next day's drinking."

All this she recited in a monotone, not a sarcastic put-down of me but a flat statement about herself. I studied her face, trying to read her feelings. When she glanced at me, our eyes met. But she seemed not there, she seemed to have left, maybe now sitting in one of those shacky double-wides with her mother.

"Aiyana, you're a beautiful young woman. Your entire future is ahead of you."

"My entire future? Two weeks before I left the trailer park everyone got notice to vacate. The gravel company bought the land. As we drove by I saw that almost everyone has packed up, their entire future lying ahead of them."

She held her half-finished hot dog in her lap and gazed into the fire in the same way she'd gazed into the flame of the lighter.

"Where will they go, Aiyana?"

"To a different double-wide in a different double-wide park, to all the same stuff as the last double-wide in the last trailer park. In other words, they go nowhere."

"Maybe the new double-wide will work better."

She fastened those black eyes on me. "Maybe the new double-wide my mother goes to will be better?"

I shrugged. "I don't know. I'm just…"

"You can't know, Eric. For you it's no more than coming into a place you don't know. But I know. So I'm asking you, please, don't take me there."

She leaned forward, her elbows on her knees, her eyes filled not with defiance now but with hopelessness. "You want to know all about me. All right. When I was ten years old I worked in the bush with Grandpa Willie. The fishing guide part was easy. I didn't feel proud of myself for finding the fish. But I had to work hard to become a knife thrower. I got to be a good knife thrower. So a few minutes ago, to impress you, I stood up and bull's-eyed twice, and for five minutes the bush-bait kid that you picked up off the street felt proud of who she was."

"And then I knocked you down for throwing my knife."

She nibbled away the last of her hot dog and, as she got up to wash her hands in the lake, she glanced across the water. "I know about knives and I know about lakes and I know about canoes. So wherever we're supposed to be going, I think we should hurry: There's a storm coming. I know about storms."

I took the binoculars from the case on my belt and scanned the far shore. Where half an hour ago the water was still and the bush silent, now whitecaps flashed and trees swayed.

I buckled my life jacket.

We launched the canoe and started off along the shore, heading for a flat-rock point jutting out shiny black in the choppy water, Aiyana hesitating every few minutes to flex her injured hand. After an hour's paddling, the threat of a storm faded as we entered the inlet and reached the cabin, nestled in its clearing on a flat-rock point.

It seemed to me that this was the first time I was seeing this scene, as though during my last trip my vision was clouded but now my vision was clear, or like last time this scene was in a smudgy frame but now the frame was clean. Stacked between two trees was a supply of split wood I hadn't noticed before. To the right, beyond the outhouse leaning askew, its door hanging open, was a hammock I had not noticed before. But to the left, exactly as I remembered, was the inlet where Julia and I had played the stone game. By the dock, exactly as I remembered, the flag rested peacefully.

Aiyana's only comment: "A Canadian flag. That's weird."

"Weird why?"

"Canadians don't put flags up anywhere. You're an American. You put flags up all over the place, especially on other people's property, especially if they've got gravel. So it should be an American flag."

Ah, I thought. That's where the hostility is coming from. Doing tricks for American CEOs. An American company taking their gravel. But I let this comment go because it was true and because, as far as Aiyana was concerned, I was one of those Americans she did knife tricks for.

I sighed. Soon this will be over. I hauled the canoe up onto the shore and led the way up the path to the front door. Here the bugs were bad, but while I waved and swatted, they didn't seem to notice Aiyana. Glancing back, I saw the lake was now flat as a mirror. In a few hours, the sun would be sinking behind the trees and then it would be dark and soon I wouldn't be able to see much of anything. So get on with the spreading of ashes and leave.

I stepped into the cabin and paused for a quick appraisal: the living room with odd furniture and stone fireplace; on the walls, snowshoes and taxidermied fish; to my right, two tiny bedrooms with lumpy mattresses and painted dressers; straight ahead, an old wooden table painted blue, two unmatched chairs, and one galvanized bucket to catch leaks when it rained. I had seen this before but now with Aiyana I seemed to be seeing it differently.

I expected a reaction from Aiyana. I expected her to be impressed at the quaintness. I expected, Wow. This is so cool.

Instead, in the exact same way Julia had entered the cabin, Aiyana walked straight into the kitchen and checked the wood stove, the cupboards, and the pump for the sink. I remembered Aiyana had done the same when she walked into the room full of Julia's stuff at Hilda's, as though she'd seen it before and was checking to make sure nothing was missing.

"Why three jars of strawberry jam?" she asked, checking the cupboard, sounding like, where did this come from?

"Julia had a thing for strawberry jam. In the middle of the night, if she was cold she'd get up and eat some strawberry jam. I wondered about that, you know, diabetes."

Aiyana stood by an open closet opposite the wood stove, examining a rifle I hadn't seen before. "This is a twelve gauge." She cracked the breach. "But Julia wasn't a hunter."

"Absolutely not. Probably belonged to her grandfather."

She reached into the closet and pulled out a box of shells. "Birdshot. Not much good for bears." She put the rifle and shells into the closet and closed the door.

It seemed peculiar that this seventeen-year-old kid would be familiar with these guns, just as it was strange that she would seem satisfied that everything was in order before she went outside to sit on the cabin's front step. The last picture Julia had shown me the last time we'd been here, her playing with the rosary, me swatting at the bugs, was of herself sitting on the exact same step.

The midafternoon sun was completing its orbit and settling itself into the trees, lingering still in patches of light on the flat rock where Julia and I had made our wishes. Aiyana got up and walked to the water's edge and began to poke along the flat-rock shoreline. She stooped to pick up and examine a small stone. She stood and half-turned toward me, standing on the edge of the flat rock, the stone clutched in her hand, standing in the same spot Julia had stood to play the game of stones. Aiyana was too far away for me to see her clearly, but it seemed to me that I could, and it seemed to me that I could see Julia clearly, standing beside her, one in the frame, the other outside the frame, but both waiting for me to scatter her ashes.

I picked up the cardboard box containing the urn, and followed the path to the water. I stood on the dock testing the direction of the wind. The sun had gone behind a single heavy cloud, and the lake was black with whitecaps farther out. Aiyana was watching a loon swimming in the calm black water of the inlet while farther out in the choppy waves, another surfaced. They mated for life, Julia had said. Maybe Aiyana's feather was from a loon. Aiyana had surfaced suddenly, appearing on the surface of my life out of nowhere, and she was definitely a little loony.

I went to the end of the dock and when I turned I saw that she had waded into the water, her long slender legs disappearing into the flat black surface, then returning, wading shoreward, standing now knee-deep. As I watched the water licking at the bare skin, I grew angry at the priest for filling her head with impossible dreams about coming to the Toronto School of Music. Dreams about being a movie star in Hollywood would have been better. She turned and, framed against the shifting backdrop of water both flat and choppy, she looked straight at me. It's time, she seemed to be saying, like that cold hand on my shoulder, that cold finger touching my arm: It's time.

I braced myself for whatever might happen next, for now the wind was gusty and unpredictable. I waited for it to turn offshore to take the ashes out across the black skin of water. Next to me, on the dock now, Aiyana waited, watching the flag that flapped and flared, responding to the wind, silent a moment when it stopped, waiting for me, it seemed, stepping up again when I turned to the water, laughing at me, it seemed, dancing a furious dance for another brief moment, skirts swirling up and twirling and then stopping abruptly, teasing me, it seemed.

Aiyana waited for me to swing the urn.

I couldn't do it. I would launch the ashes into the air just at precisely the wrong moment, and the wind would shift and blow them back in my face.

She said, "Let me do it."

She took the urn and removed the lid. There was no wind and no breeze and no sun. The water was flat and black and the flag hung silent as Aiyana swung back her arm and, at the precise moment the wind picked up, she cast the ashes. Her timing was perfect. The dust in the wind sailed out across the waiting water.

She peered into the urn. "Not quite," she said. The wind fell silent again, waiting for her signal. She swung the urn again, and the wind stepped up again to dance its dance and swirl its skirts, taking the last of Julia away.

Aiyana took my hand and she turned my back to the water and returned me to the cabin. My emotions a tangle, I sat at the table. "Where will she go?" I surprised myself by asking the question, as though I now thought Aiyana had released her and sent her with the wind to wherever she should be.

"The currents will take her to the other side."

"What other side?"

She sat opposite me, her deep black eyes searching mine. "Julia is gone. What will you do now, Eric?"

She sat opposite me on one of the old wooden chairs, a yellow one that matched nothing, except maybe the pump handle of the sink but I couldn't tell for sure. She was staring at me, her eyes full of sympathy, her finger ready to wipe away the tears that should have been coming but weren't.

What will I do now that nothing is matching anything? I will go home to an empty apartment and go into an empty bedroom and lie down in an empty bed and think about the dance of that flag.

"A storm is coming," she reminded me. "Best leave, be on our way."

Otherwise, an overnight in this cabin — and all night long that spooky call: *Where are you?*

She said softly, "She's gone, Eric."

Gone? Julia did not settle quietly into dreamless dark, me at her side as she slipped into eternal peace. That part of Julia that was mineral had turned back into mineral, and that part of her that was water had turned back into water. But that part of her that was her had turned into something indefinable, staring at me from just beneath the black bottomless eyes of the one across from me. The Julia who only three months ago had lain in the dreamless dark of the roadside ditch would soon be lying in the dream-filled dark of my bedroom. I could see it, me clutching at her arm. I could see it, I could see myself, shaking her awake, asking this girl Aiyana, not "*Where* are you," but "*Who* are you…"

Aiyana put her hand on mine. "She's gone. And now it's time for us to go."

If she was gone, why was I still feeling her here?

I got up. I went into the bedroom and sat on the iron-framed bed. Aiyana came in and sat beside me.

I asked her, "What should I do with the urn?"

"Leave it here."

"I can't."

"You can't take her with you."

"I must."

She shook her head, her lips a tight no. But I picked up the urn and carried it to the canoe.

CHAPTER SIXTEEN

Eric

Now the lake was perfectly calm, a flat blue in the late-afternoon sun that had moved away the clouds and cleared the sky. It didn't look like any storm was coming. We set off. She was still not wearing a life jacket. After every three or four strokes, she stopped paddling and flexed the fingers of her injured hand.

She asked, "Have you ever wondered what it feels like to drown?"

Her voice seemed so pensive she could've been talking to herself. And why ask me this? Did she think that was what Julia must feel like right now?

"When I found my father, his eyes were still open, looking up at me."

We were in the spot where Julia's ashes should now be floating, if not on the surface then suspended halfway down, right below me. I leaned over and looked down to see if I could see her. Or maybe they were still airborne, and if I turned and looked up I would see her following me.

Aiyana stopped paddling to flex her fingers and rub her wrist. "My grandfather told me, in the old days in the winter, the Aboriginals took their dead out to the centre of Broken Deer Lake and left them on the ice because in the spring the currents would take them to the spirit world on the other side."

"What other side?"

"Sometimes they'd find the bodies washed up on the shore when the ice melted. That meant they hadn't gone to the spirit world yet, over the River Styx to the land of souls, and they needed to complete the ceremony."

I stopped paddling, for a moment so convinced Julia had not sunk to the bottom or got picked up by any undercurrent but had washed up on shore that I almost called, "Where are you?" I couldn't help it.

Aiyana continued. "After my father died, fell through the ice, I got nightmares that came from the other side. I'd look up and over the lake, thinking my father would be coming back any moment. Because whenever he waved goodbye, he always came back. But he didn't come back. So I started looking for him for real when April came, when the ice was coming out, and one morning I saw that the ice was boiling up in one spot, so I was watching and waiting at that spot. As the ice began to drift, I followed the underwater currents; different currents are different colours under the ice. So I followed the currents and I found him washed up on shore, still frozen, his hands when I touched them ice cold. It was him, yes, but some other him, like there were two hims, with different-coloured faces, and the one I had found had no colour, like mushrooms. The one I remembered had lots of colour, like lots of energy. I didn't understand. In early May the loons came back and every night I listened to their call coming from the other side, *Where are you? Where are you?* So I knew the other him was still out there, on the lake, calling for me from the other side."

I couldn't help asking again, "What other side?"

But just then the wind picked up, so the question I needed an answer for was snatched away from me. And after that she remained silent, and I feared the answer she had given would not be given again, so I would probably never know. But then, I thought, I don't want to know. I am an accountant. Numbers I could understand, accounts I could figure out, balance sheets I could add up and get an answer for. Audits were in proper columns, sums were at the bottom of each sheet with an answer that applied to the question. That is what I was good at. My head was full of numbers. I was comfortable with numbers and that is how I wanted it.

We followed the rocky point away from the shore. In the open, the wind stayed strong, turning the water into whitecaps. She stopped paddling to loosen her fingers and her wrist. She was looking beyond the end of the point where the whitecaps had turned into high swells that she was intentionally paddling into.

I called to her, "It's too rough. We have to turn back."

But the wind became stronger and the canoe began to reel as wave after wave smashed upon us, covering us with cold spray. I tried to turn shoreward, but the wind, booming down from the end of the lake, pushed the canoe farther out where black water churned itself white. When one long rolling swell picked us up broadside, throwing us off balance, we spilled into the water.

I came up behind the canoe, which was upside down between the paddles, which were floating a few feet beyond Aiyana, already on their way to the opposite shore.

I called to her, "Where's your life jacket?"

It was floating away, rising and falling with the swell of the water. She kicked off and swam away, after her life jacket I thought.

"Stay with the canoe, Aiyana!" I had watched the safety video.

But she swam on, appearing and disappearing in the fall and rise of the waves. I recovered the paddles and when I looked again, she had disappeared. Hoisting myself up on one end of the canoe, I searched the swells and whitecaps. I slipped back into the water, kicked away, riding the waves upward out of each trough to the crest, looking for her. But between the patches of white, the lake was black and empty, except for the red bobbing bottom of the canoe that was now on its way to the opposite shoreline. I turned away from it.

She's made it to shore, I decided. I swam on, reaching the shallows so suddenly I cut my finger as my hands scraped across the gravelly bottom. I stood up in ankle-deep water and scanned the trees of the shoreline, which curved gradually into rocks jutting out to a long point. I couldn't see her. Beyond the point, dense bush, thick as a jungle, grew to the water's edge. Carefully, I picked my way through the stones along the shore and called for her but there was no answer.

I sank down on a rock and buried my head in my hands as my tangled emotions threatened to unravel. I was not huddled in the roadside ditch, the cold breeze from the cornfield behind me whispering accusations in my ear. I was sitting on the shoreline, the cold water from the lake slashing accusations against my bare ankles. I knew if I sat there long enough and waited long enough and looked close enough, I would eventually see both of them, Aiyana and Julia, floating there at my feet.

As I removed my waterlogged sneakers and socks, the cut finger leaked thin ribbons of red into the water. I could feel in that finger the shadowy foam rushing forward to the shore and then retreating the way the wind in that flag had stepped up and stepped back and retreated. Then, as I turned to get up, Aiyana stepped forward from the trees, her long hair clinging in wet strands to either side of her face.

"What happened to you?" I asked. "I thought you drowned."

"The urn. It's gone. These lakes are thirty feet deep."

I said nothing. I pulled on my shoes and followed her. She seemed to know where she was going, so I knew this lake was familiar, that she knew all about it. I followed her along the shore, picking my way over the wet stones. When her right foot slipped, twisting the broken sandal and breaking another strap, I crouched at her feet to try to fix it. I saw that her toes, like her fingers, were long and slender. Then I saw that her foot was covered with a pale gritty dust that, when I tried to wipe it off, felt like grey ash.

She was staring down at me. "Get up. We have to go."

I felt the ash on my fingers. I watched each grain of black grit creep up the back of my hand to fasten a grip around my arm.

"Eric, what are you doing?" She pulled her foot away from me. "Let go of it. We have to go. She's gone."

I could taste the smoke of burned flesh filling my mouth, overflowing as I coughed and spit it onto the rocks.

Aiyana stepped back. "That's gross. Stop it. She had to go."

We continued along the shore, Aiyana carrying the sandal in her left hand. At the Wrangler, I opened the glove compartment for my first-aid kit. I attempted to wrap the cut finger but had difficulty holding the tape. Aiyana took it and began to wrap the cut.

The wind had died and the clouds had gone and the sun was out and she was bandaging the cut. As she worked, I saw bits of ash mixed with glints of sunlight that danced and swirled in the drops of lake water suspended in the long black hair at her shoulders. When she finished, I saw these same bits of ash floating in the black of her eyes as she looked straight at me.

She dropped my hand but did not shift her eyes away from mine. I was looking right at her, trying to see into her, like opening endless sliding doors of water, trying to reach that urn lying on the bottom. But no sooner did I step through one and get a glimpse of it, there was another to keep me locked out. She stepped back and turned aside as if to say, I haven't yet given you permission to look at me and see me and find out who I now am.

...

Aiyana sat slouched in her seat in the Wrangler biting her nails in silence as we followed the gravel road to the stop sign at Highway 69. To the left were the Broken Deer Lakes. To the right was Toronto.

Aiyana broke the silence. "You are caught between here and there the same as I am."

"What do you mean, between here and there?"

"I don't know about you. For me it's here and there. *Here* is wrong time and wrong notes. *There* is right time and right notes. At least I know where I am. But you, now you're like a … a dog with too many smells, some here, some there, you can't sort them out."

The Wrangler was idling.

"You can take me home, but I'll come back. For Socks, of course. But also I promised Father Clark I would try out for Juilliard, and I have to keep my promise."

"Juilliard? Yesterday you were here for piano lessons and now you think you're going to Juilliard? Aiyana. Give your head a shake!"

She sank further into her slouch. She said flatly, "For me to take piano lessons, Eric, would be like a fish taking swimming lessons."

"You said piano lessons with Dr. McCoy. Why are you now saying Juilliard?"

The Wrangler was waiting for the blinker to give it directions.

She shrugged. "I started playing when I was four. We lived in Sudbury then. We had a piano then, from a neighbour. My father couldn't play it, but he'd use it as an excuse to get me away from the kids who were picking on me. He'd call from the front door, 'Aiyana, let's play the piano.' He hooked me with the *play* part. If I couldn't play with the other kids, I could play with him on the piano. Then he drowned and my mother moved to Broken Deer Double-Wides, and the kids there picked on me and wouldn't let me play with them so I did my playing with Father Clark on the piano in the church basement. But by then, I had taught myself how to play the piano."

The Wrangler was idling, waiting.

"But that doesn't mean you can just decide to go to Juilliard."

"I promised Father Clark, so I will."

When she put her hand to her mouth to bite at her nails, I took it. I placed the hand in her lap. I turned south on 69, and we drove in silence to the 400. We stopped at Tim Hortons for a sandwich and continued in silence for the rest of the way, reaching the Wilson house at 12:35 a.m.

Aiyana went immediately up the stairs to bed. I wondered if tonight she would wear Julia's pyjamas, although I did not know why I would wonder that. In this hot weather Julia would not have worn pyjamas. Sitting in the recliner, I must have dropped off to sleep, for when she tapped on my door to ask if it was okay if she had a snack of strawberry jam and could she wear this pair of pyjamas because she was cold, I remembered Julia always made herself a snack of strawberry jam when she felt cold and couldn't sleep. Then it occurred to me that the bottom of the lake was ice cold. Then it occurred to me I must be having a dream.

CHAPTER SEVENTEEN

Aiyana

Gifted. That was the word the Sudbury church ladies used when they brought boxes of clothes to the Broken Deer church. That meant that even if they didn't fit, you couldn't take them back. Unless they agreed to take them back. So I knew that whatever clothes I'd already taken from Julia I could not give back. Plus all her winter stuff. I would have to keep that too.

The wearing of other people's clothes was nothing new for me. My mother got mine at the clothing bank in All Saints' Church in Little Deer. Millie George's mother did too. Jimmy George would wear second-hand stuff but not pyjamas because the person who used to sleep in them would come back at night to haunt him in his dreams, and he could prove it, he said. Hartley never wore pyjamas. He looked like he never slept. And he looked like he got his clothes from the morgue.

Sometimes Father Clark bought me new pyjamas at Walmart and took the tags off and dropped them off at our trailer and said to my mother, "This got left on my doorstep. It looks like it might fit Aiyana. And here's some strawberry jam that looks like it's never been opened."

I wasn't thinking about wearing Julia's pyjamas as I sorted through her jeans and shorts and sweaters, hats, and mitts. And I wasn't thinking of Julia as a dead person. I was remembering my mother would sit at the table and eat the strawberry jam she got at the food bank. On her toast. I could hear her, my mother, spreading a dead person's strawberry jam on her toast. So then I would hear my mother's boyfriends sitting in my father's chair chewing and smacking their lips, gobbling up the strawberry jam, so then I would hear the dead people the strawberry jam belonged to in the first place come in from the other side to gobble up the strawberry jam before it was all gone.

Then I remembered I had noticed strawberry jam sitting in Eric's fridge, and I remembered Eric saying Julia ate strawberry jam when she was cold and where she was now was definitely cold. So then I knew if I didn't throw that strawberry jam away she would be coming up at night from the bottom of the lake to sit at Eric's kitchen table to eat the strawberry jam.

The churches in the South sent nursery-rhyme books to the churches in the North as gifts. Millie George, giggling and squirming in her chair, read the stories to me: "Mary had a little lamb, her father shot it dead. Now it goes to school with her, between two hunks of bread." This was just a silly story. The strawberry jam wasn't. That's how things come to me and that's why I threw Julia's strawberry jam away.

...

When I heard the tap-tap on Hilda's apartment door, I went to the front window to look out. There were no signs of Hartley's car. And Hartley would not tap-tap. I slid back the chain lock.

Eric said, "Did you still want to go to the university to find out about McCoy? And about your money?"

Madison Avenue looked like the tree-lined streets in the little town where Dr. Roberts from my TV show lived. The big square brick houses looked like his house. On his front lawn was a sign: Dr. B. B. Roberts. Physician. I couldn't read it but I knew what it said. His office was through a side door and down the stairs to a waiting room where Mrs. Roberts answered the phone and made the appointments.

The secretary at the faculty looked like Dr. Roberts's wife, middle-aged with a warm smile and a cardigan that sagged at the pockets. She didn't know how to contact Dr. McCoy in Ireland and knew nothing about Father Clark sending money. "The music programs here at the university are for our enrolled students. You need a high school diploma and references from your previous music program. Where did you go to high school, Aiyana?"

"I never went to school."

Eric said, "What? You never went to school?"

The secretary said, "You must have gone to school somewhere, a music program of some sort."

"I'm from up north," I said. "My priest made arrangements with Dr. McCoy. He knows about it."

"I'm sure he'll be back in September. Perhaps come back at the end of the summer."

"Where she lived up north she couldn't attend school," Eric said. "She's had a difficult home life. Up north."

The secretary glanced at my chewed fingernails. "I'm sorry. You'll have to wait for Dr. McCoy. He's not answering our emails right now. He's off on personal leave and doesn't want to be disturbed."

We left the university. I stared at the students coming and going along the sidewalk in the morning sunshine, crossing at the lights, some in pairs holding hands, disappearing into buildings filled with people who had gone to school and could read and write and tell the time. I thought, if I were any one of those students, I could go back to Eric's place and write my story in a book as thick as a Bible and give it to this secretary who would read it and think, this person deserves a chance. She would give it to one of those music professors who would read it and say, this girl deserves a chance.

Eric seemed like a decent person. He didn't stare at me with a hooters look. He probably didn't know what bush bait meant. Whatever age he was, twenty-seven maybe, he'd probably had a sheltered rich-boy private-school life, like the son of those rich CEOs Grandpa Willie and me took fishing. So I was surprised when, coming to my defence, he had said, "Where she lived up north she couldn't attend school. She's had a difficult home life. Up north."

So walking along Madison, I was more surprised when, like taking an interest in me, he said, "One thing I noticed, the secretary was looking at your hands and what she saw was the bloody fingernails. We must look after the nail-biting. It's like you're punishing yourself, destroying what's most important to you, chewing your fingers till they bleed all over the piano keys. You're a Catholic, Aiyana. Is this some kind of crucifixion nail-through-your-palm thing?"

But then, when he said, "Your dream is to be a pianist. I know but…"

I prepared myself for a running-away-from-home-to-take-piano-lessons scolding. I glanced at him, waiting for it.

"So … yeah. Keep your dream inside, hang on to it. Memories fade away, but not dreams. But, I gotta say, Aiyana, this faculty-of-music idea that this up-north priest has put in your head is not making any sense."

Him saying this, as I walked along Madison Avenue, sounded like he thought I was someone from the dark side of the moon.

CHAPTER EIGHTEEN

Eric

I was awakened by her tugging at my arm. "He's here. Wake up." Aiyana was standing by my bed, dressed in Julia's pyjamas.

"Who's here?"

"Hartley," she whispered. "Outside."

Through the bedroom window, I saw the gleaming chrome and paint of his newborn Caddy glinting beneath the street lamp. Hartley stepped out. He stood by the front fender, looking at the house. Then he started up the walk.

Aiyana fastened the chain lock on the apartment door and came back into the bedroom. "Where can I hide?"

"The front door is locked. He can't get in."

But the front door opened. We'd forgotten to snap the dead bolt.

Hartley's work boots clumped along the hall. A light blinked on and a sliver of white appeared beneath my door. It rattled, then the footsteps moved on, climbing the stairs to Hilda's.

"I didn't lock it," Aiyana whispered. "He's going to find my stuff."

When I heard the upper door open, I looked at the ceiling, following his muffled footfalls on the broadloom as he crossed into Hilda's kitchen. For a moment all was quiet. Then they resumed, coming down and along the outer hall to my door. When it rattled, Aiyana clutched my arm.

Hartley knocked two knocks. "Your mother wants you back home. I know you're in there, Aiyana."

Her grip on my arm tightened.

"Open up this damn door or I'll break it down!"

A moment's silence was followed by a crash as either his shoulder or his foot hit the wood, and the lock sprang open. But the chain held. Hartley forced in his hand as far as his knuckles but, unable to reach farther, he drew back and a second crash shook the door. Still the chain held.

"Aiyana!" At the bark of her name, she flinched. "Your cat's here so I know you're here."

I motioned for Aiyana to hide in the bedroom closet and I opened the apartment door halfway. From Hartley's lanky frame hung the rumpled plaid shirt and baggy blue work pants. He glared at me. "Who are you anyway?"

"Eric Cooper."

"I'm looking for Aiyana. Where is she?"

"There's no one here called Aiyana."

"The guy next door said he saw her here." Hartley hunched forward, the stench of cigarettes and alcohol floating in as I peered out. He placed nicotine-stained fingers against the door and pushed. I planted one foot against the door. Hartley craned his neck and looked over my shoulder into the living room. I leaned into the door, attempting to close it. Hartley leaned back with equal weight, and the door didn't move.

He said, "She shouldn't have run off the way she did." Hartley stepped sideways, trying to see beyond the living room. "Her mother wants her back home. She's worried sick."

"Well, she's not here. I can't help you." I leaned my full weight against the door and managed to click it shut.

"I'm going to check this out!" Hartley hollered. "If you're in there, Aiyana, I'll be back."

Hartley thumped away. From the bedroom window, we watched him cut across the grass and climb into his Caddy. The Caddy pulled away from the curb. As it rumbled up the street, I noticed Hartley had added dual-exhaust chrome extensions to his American boat.

Aiyana said, "He'll be back. I know he will." She was sitting on the bed, biting her nails. "What are we going to do? What if he comes back?"

"We'll keep the doors locked."

"Locks! Locks don't mean anything to Hartley!"

She was right. If Hartley returned for a second attack, that door probably wouldn't hold. "We'll call the police."

"They'll phone Children's Aid. I'll be eighteen in two weeks. Then we phone the police." She curled one long strand of hair around her index finger. Her voice barely above a whisper, she asked, "Can I sleep here tonight?"

"Here? With me? In this bed?"

"Not with you." Her face flushed and she glared at me. "Not with you. On the floor."

I pulled off the top blanket and handed it to her and, as she curled up under the blanket on the floor, I climbed into bed. I turned off the light and stared at the ceiling. I sighed. "This isn't right."

She stood watching me, one arm across her chest, one hand fretting with her hair, as I switched my sheets to the couch and fitted fresh sheets on the bed for her. I sat in the recliner and tilted it back and listened to the soft whispers of her breathing coming from my bedroom.

···

In the morning, while I made the coffee, Aiyana stripped and folded my bedding and, without asking, put it on the foot of my bed, ready for my next night on the couch, like establishing a his-and-hers permanent situation, me near the door, her in my bed.

Wearing Julia's bathrobe, she sat at the piano, flexing her fingers. While she ran the scales, I poured some Nature's Best into her bowl and mine. I tried to remember if there was a hardware store nearby so I could buy a chain lock for the front door.

I had planned to work all day on Julia's will. I wasn't familiar with Canadian intestate laws, but I was familiar with the way governments worked: slowly and incompetently. I'd told the lawyer I'd look after Julia's debts, but I didn't know how extensive they were or how many endless forms I would need to sign. I anticipated that almost every transaction would require a phone call that involved being on hold for an hour.

But when Aiyana said, "I found this in Hilda's apartment," I decided all this could wait. She gave me a glossy three-page Hudson's Bay flyer for women's summer wear.

"I still have the two hundred dollars I brought with me."

"Well, okay. While I sit in Starbucks, you wander around the mall, pick up what you need."

"What I need is decent clothes so that tomorrow or the next day, as soon as my hand is feeling better, I can go back to the university, sit down in the Faculty of Music office, and refuse to leave until someone listens to me play. If Dr. McCoy isn't there, some other doctor of music will be. I don't need certificates or diplomas. All I need is for them to hear me play."

I hesitated about telling her the truth about Father Clark's cheque, but now seemed like a good time. "It'll be legal tender if he had a will. But even still, there are a hundred forms to fill out before the bank will cash it. It could take months."

She got up and stood looking out the window, choosing not to hear me, it seemed.

I said, "What I mean is, if you're worried about the money, don't be. I can lend you some."

"It's not just clothes. I need new sandals." Then she added, "I know you said I could have Julia's stuff, but it doesn't fit right."

I thought, Aiyana is a seventeen-year-old kid. Last night she slept in my bed. Now she is wearing Julia's bathrobe. In a few minutes we'll be eating breakfast together. Added to that ten minutes ago the scarecrow boyfriend tried to break down the door. If new clothes will help get her out of here and into the university and on her way to wherever, new clothes it is. "Then we go to Payless and to the Bay. The Bay and Payless."

...

As we drove up Madison, the late-morning sun beating down on the roof of the Wrangler, I tried to think of a mall closer than Yorkdale to avoid the traffic. But then, I reasoned, it would be a straight run across the 401 to the Allen, so Yorkdale was probably as good as any.

Aiyana pulled back her hair so the AC could blow on her face. She tugged at the bottom of the too-small wolf-stencilled Wildlife Society t-shirt and tried to tuck it into the too-big Julia shorts. She said, "Most of the stuff in the flyer looked like bush bait, but the designer jeans with the three-pack of ribbed t-shirts looked nice."

The traffic up Avenue Road was slow. By now it was getting close to lunchtime; Yorkdale would be a nightmare. What I thought would take two hours was going to take half a day. But I didn't comment, not even after twenty minutes of stop-and-go from St. Clair to Eglinton, Aiyana worrying her nails the entire way.

I was worried about Hartley. He didn't look like a break-and-enter cat burglar dressed in black tights on his way to a midnight theft. They wore night-vision goggles and swung from balconies ten stories up, opening safes and stealing jewellery. And he didn't look like a gangster. He looked like a drunk Ichabod Crane. But Aiyana had mentioned he had a gun. My instincts were telling me he'd have it with him when he returned.

Yorkdale was under construction. Half the parking area was blocked off, and a mile-high crane sat near the Bay entrance. I drove around for a few minutes looking for a parking spot and finally stopped near the entrance. "You go on your own. Come back in an hour. I'll be somewhere around the crane."

As Aiyana got out of the Wrangler, a woman got out the car beside us. Her red dress and squat body leaning forward in a short-legged flat-out march across the asphalt reminded me of my grade-three teacher, Miss Pinch, who was also my Sunday school teacher. Aiyana followed the red dress for a few steps, her long legs one step to the woman's two, until she passed the Miss Pinch lookalike and disappeared into the mall.

Too late, I remembered Aiyana had no watch. Well, she could ask someone. Then I remembered Julia hadn't been wearing her watch when I rolled, so it was probably in her jewellery drawer where she kept her earrings and bracelets. I could give it to Aiyana. I'd seen the thin gold necklace with the tiny cross in there too, in a tiny snap-open velvet box. I had taken it out to see if it was the same as the one in her grad photo; it was. I wasn't thinking of giving these things to Aiyana, like clothes. Clothes had no value. You gave clothes to charity. But not jewellery. This was different. So was I thinking of using Aiyana to get rid of Julia's jewellery, or was I thinking of giving the jewellery as a gift?

A man loaded with parcels and two children was coming along the asphalt. I pulled closer and signalled my intention. When the car finally pulled out, I pulled in and shut off the Wrangler.

I checked my watch. She'd been gone half an hour. If Aiyana had a cellphone, I could have given her my location, opposite the crane. I would give her Julia's cellphone. To get rid of it.

Above the crane, the sun, partly obscured by a smoky haze of fluffy clouds, was a crimson ball shading from red to yellow around the edges. Sitting here with me now, Julia would say, "Look at the sun. Look at the colours. It looks nice but it isn't. Air pollution turns the atmosphere into clouds that drop polluted rain into our lakes and rivers." This reminded me that there could be no way Julia would have wanted her remains to go from that chimney into clouds of black carbon to pollute the air, and there is no way Julia would have wanted her ashes to add more pollution to the lakes and rivers. Lakes and rivers made me think of Aiyana, who in a few moments would surface wearing her own clothes and not Julia's, and I could get on with my life instead of every time I saw the one, my mind went to the other.

I found her standing by the crane empty-handed in the same Wolf Society outfit she'd arrived in. She did not look at me. "I don't want to talk about it. I want to go home."

She crossed the asphalt, and I followed. She sat beside me in the front seat and stared at her hands lying open in her lap. She flexed the fingers and rubbed the wrist. She raised the good hand to move one long strand of hair from her face, the scabbed fingers straying along her cheek before dropping down to join the other, now resting on the hem of her wolf t-shirt. "No one at the Bay would help me," she said. "I went to another store. I stood there waiting for someone to help me. But people were just staring at me. So I started to cry."

"Cry? Why? Did someone say something to you?"

Aiyana glanced at her hands. "It's going to sound stupid, I know, but when we had concerts at the school in Big Deer, when I played the piano in front of everyone, I always felt weird because the other kids wore knee socks that matched but my knee socks never matched." She looked at me. "That's what I remember most. Mismatched socks. In that store, standing by the socks, it was like I was little again, like I was back home again, like I was the trailer-park kid with mismatched knee socks."

"So you didn't buy anything, not even socks?"

"No one would help me."

"But socks come already matched."

"I didn't want socks. I wanted other stuff. I had pictures. Three decent t-shirts and one pair of designer jeans and maybe a blouse and cargo pants. But no one would help me and everything else I looked at was bush bait."

She seemed to have a thing about bush bait, which I figured was the name for pick-up girls in the trailer park, which she was definitely not.

"So you left."

She stared out the window, tears now streaming down her cheeks.

I pulled out of the parking lot and drove south on Dufferin. I was trying to be gentle when I said, "It's a mall. Sometimes in those stores it's hard to find someone to help you. How about Payless? What happened there?"

"I couldn't find Payless."

"Aiyana, there are signs for the mall layout. They have an arrow that says You Are Here and then you find the name Payless. Then you go and find what you want."

She said, "What could be easier?"

"Exactly. What could be easier?"

"What did you say?" Her eyes glittered anger.

"I just said what you said."

"I heard what you said. What could be easier?"

I remained calm. "It's called shopping, Aiyana."

"It's called what could be easier."

I kept driving, waiting for her to resume her attack, but her face softened. The scabby fingers came up to worry the strand of hair. She turned away, wiped her eyes with the back of her fingers. "Father Clark tried to help me. The disability teacher tried to help me. 'What letter is this, Aiyana? What letter is that, Aiyana?'"

"But there are signs all over the place."

"Signs, Eric? Signs? I can't follow signs. Don't you get it? I couldn't find the stores because I couldn't read the words. I don't know how much anything costs because I can't read numbers. I couldn't find Payless on the signboard because I can't read maps." Her voice was rising. "'What could be easier?' you said. I must be stupid. You were calling me stupid. I wasn't being stupid. I was being dyslexic. I can't read."

When we got home she went straight up to Hilda's and changed into a pair of Julia's jeans and black V-neck sweater. She came back to my apartment, picked up her purse, and slipped it over her shoulder.

"Can you feed Socks for me? There's cat food in the fridge."

"Where are you going?"

"The university. I'm going to the Faculty of Music and I won't leave until they listen to me play. I'm going to sit there all night if I have to."

"You can't do that. Security will make you leave."

Her eyes, filled with determination, met mine for a moment before shifting away. She retreated to the recliner and began to fix her hair. Her hair obsession seemed to be like her nail-biting obsession. Like a security thing. Like her cat. Like that lighter. And I realized in a sudden light-bulb moment, like the piano-playing obsession.

I glanced up. From the wall above, Julia stared at me from her grad photo, her face and neck so pale that her thin gold chain was barely visible. I went upstairs to Hilda's apartment where I rummaged through the dresser drawer, finally finding the small velvet box. I snapped it open. Julia's necklace and its tiny cross lay in a red silk nest. I returned to my apartment and handed Aiyana the velvet box. "Julia always wore this with that V-neck sweater."

Aiyana took the box. Her chewed fingers picked up the gold necklace.

"I'll go with you to the university and stay with you until someone will listen to you play. But first, we get your fingers and your wrist better, and I mean totally better. In the meantime, you and I go to Yorkdale tomorrow and I'll take you to whatever store you want and make sure you get whatever you need."

For the very first time since she had appeared out of nowhere on my doorstep Aiyana smiled.

We went to Forever 21. Aiyana picked through ladies' wear while I stood to one side. I waited while she went into the change room. I felt awkward standing there, Aiyana waiting for my approval, which was always, "You look beautiful."

I didn't feel right saying beautiful. I felt like I was being … I don't know. Too familiar. But even wearing only jeans and a t-shirt and never any makeup that I could tell, she truly was beautiful. When she glanced up and caught me watching her as she selected two pairs of cropped khakis and two sleeveless tops and two sweaters to go with two pair of designer jeans and a pair of summer pyjamas, I felt embarrassed. There is looking and there is seeing and there is watching. She was truly beautiful.

After we got new sandals at Payless, we went along the mall to the food court. She sat at one of the tables, her hand and wrist in the lap of her new designer jeans, while I lined up for the hot dogs. As I sat down, I said, "Now you've been shopping in the big city. How does it feel?"

She thought about it. "I was prepared for Toronto with the shopping malls, the skyscrapers, the traffic jams — because I'd seen all this on TV. But the garbage containers surprised me. Everywhere there's different-coloured bins with pictures on the front for different garbage, as though lots of people in this city can't read. Everywhere in the mall there's different-coloured faces, mismatched people like mismatched socks."

I said, "And now with new sandals, like Cinderella getting a glass slipper."

She smiled. Her second smile. Smiling eyes even.

CHAPTER NINETEEN

Eric

The walls of the office at the Second Chance Literacy Counsel were lined with hardcover texts about reading disabilities. Valerie led me into her office. "So how do I teach her to read and write and tell time?"

Valerie answered, "Well it's not going to be easy."

"She's sharp as a whip. The way she talks ... she could make Obama look slow."

"Some dyslexics have the gift of oratory. To quote my literacy teacher, 'Because they're tone-deaf to letters, they learn to sing a symphony with words. I'm not surprised she's smart. The brain of a person with dyslexia will process hundreds of combinations of just a few letters in the blink of an eye. If she can recognize the word dog, for example, it's because she can hook all these variations into one concrete symbol in her brain. But trigger words like *maybe* or *perhaps* have no hooks. They don't correspond to any concrete symbol. There's no picture, so they come up blank. Numbers are the same."

"So how do I teach her numbers and ... and these trigger words?"

"Maybe you can, maybe you can't. I can lend you some flashcards."

Valerie opened her bottom drawer and brought out a bundle of white cards. "You start with the Dolch sight list, the two hundred fifty most commonly used words. If she can learn these by sight, come back and see me and we'll move to phonics."

. . .

I found Aiyana in Julia's recliner watching Dr. Roberts reruns. I didn't understand her obsession with this show, other than it represented a wholesome family from the fifties, something she never had. But I now understood that this pattern of obsessions seemed to keep her grounded.

"Aiyana, I want to show you these flashcards, see how many you know. The ones you don't, I'm going to teach you."

"Teach me what, exactly?" She was concentrating on Dr. Roberts, not paying attention to me.

"I got these cards from an adult literacy agency. They help—"

"Disabled people?"

"Not just disabled but—"

"I can't learn," she said simply. "I'm dyslexic." She pointed the remote and turned up the volume.

"You can learn. Come over here and read these for me so I know where to start." I laid the cards on the dining room table.

"Where you start is you don't start. Father Clark tried to teach me. I learned the alphabet and three words: cat, dog, piano. And Dr. Roberts."

I shut off Dr. Roberts. "I'm trying to help you."

"So you're a missionary now?" She picked up the remote and turned on Dr. Roberts.

"Will you go with me to the literacy agency for an assessment?"

"No."

"Why not? Don't you want to l—"

"Maybe if I could spell, I'd be able to spell it out for you."

"Would you drop the attitude? I want to help you."

She glared at me. "You want to put me in a chair and put all the words on those little cards into my brain."

"If you won't let me teach you, I'll pay for lessons at the agency."

"Put me in a chair and put all these words into my brain because I'm disabled."

I was determined to stay calm. I held up one card and pointed to the word *up*.

"It's just lines."

"All right. Like on a map. Start with lines."

"I can't read maps."

I drew a breath and sighed. I refused to lose patience. I went into the bedroom and returned with a sheet of paper. "I'm going to draw lines. For example, the cabin is up here, near the top. See? Here's north. It's near the top. We started down here."

"If you need to go again, I know how to get there."

"A straight line up to the cabin." I sorted through the cards until I found an uppercase letter I. "What is it?"

"A line."

"Good, okay. The letter I is a line." I drew a lake around the line. "What is that?"

"A lake, and if you follow the line you get to the cabin. But why do you want to go again?"

"So I take this line out of the lake and put it beside the lake, what letter is it?"

She stared at the cards. "The government sent up a psychologist who arranged the inkblot cards for the FAS kids. She asked them, 'What do you see?' They saw snakes, zombies, devils, and monsters. The psychologist went home."

"And?"

"And nothing. She wrote a report. She gave it to the president."

"You don't have a president; you have a prime minister."

"Then that's where she went wrong. She should have given it to the prime minister."

"Why are you making fun of me?"

She stared at the cards. "I know you want to help, but it's when you put the letters together, I can't read them. Letters and maps, I don't see anything but lines, some straight, some curved."

"Good. Okay. Better than monsters." I held up the card again. "What letter is it?"

She sighed. "If I go out in the grass and drag my feet around and make a bunch of lines and circles and then I say to you, 'What does this say?' you won't know. Just lines and circles in the grass. Maps are the same. I can't make sense of them. I'm an anomaly, they said."

"You're not an anomaly. You're dyslexic."

"She's weird. Lock her up in an ice hut." She was smiling a little, teasing me.

"But you speak better than most people I know. How did that happen?"

"Watching Dr. Roberts."

"Okay, forget about the map." I turned over the paper. "Forget about the flashcards." I gathered them up and put them on the bookshelf. "Just come with me to the agency."

"No."

"I'll make you a deal. If you take literacy lessons, I'll pay for piano lessons, the best money can buy."

"Piano lessons?"

"Please, Aiyana."

"Piano lessons?" She picked up the cat, which was asleep on the chesterfield. She went down the hall and up the stairs and slammed the door of Hilda's apartment.

I sat back down at the table. Maybe I should go upstairs and tap on her door and apologize for being insensitive. But she saved me the trouble. She came back and sat in the recliner, slipped off her new sandals, and rubbed her foot. She'd painted her toenails pink. Julia rarely bothered with her toenails, but when she did, the colour was pink. In fact, that was probably Julia's.

Aiyana was wearing her new jeans but the top was Julia's Greenpeace t-shirt. She'd pulled her hair back in some kind of braided bun so her hair looked short. At the back of her neck, a thin bar of light from the lamp beside the chair fell in a line of sparkles along Julia's thin gold chain. She sat there, eyes closed, hands clasped in her lap like she was praying. Or like she was listening. She must have sensed I was focused on her. She said, eyes still closed, "There's something about me you have to understand. I can't take piano lessons. I can't read notes. I can't understand music theory. I don't understand sharps and flats and bass and treble. Please don't talk to me about taking piano lessons. I'm a freak of nature. As well as a few other freaky things, I'm a musical savant."

She opened her eyes and studied her hands the way she'd studied the flame of the lighter. "My fingers are better. I'm ready to go to the Faculty of Music. And I'll sit there until someone hears my music."

"Do you want me to come?

She shook her head.

"Then let me write down my phone number. Give it to the policeman when you get arrested."

From my bedroom window, I watched her disappear down the street in one of Julia's cowl-neck dresses. I opened my computer and googled *the musical savant.* Like a good accountant, I made notes as I read through the topic:

- *savants like Leslie Lemke and Derek Paravicini could play complex piano concertos after hearing them only once.*
- *some savants play without any training what was considered impossible for any professional pianist*
- *seem to come preprogrammed for musical genius*
- *instantly grasp what would be considered impossible for the ordinary brain*

I googled *savant.*

- *some seem to possess "dual citizenship" in two parallel realities — the normal and the paranormal*
- *these "paranormal" individuals have an intuitive intelligence functioning outside the boundaries of the individual mind*

studies have identified a gene — VMAT2 — as the DNA marker of savants who can bridge the two parallel levels of consciousness, material and mystical: a phenomenon called acausal parallelism

I was interrupted by a phone call from a Mrs. Bond, the receptionist at the Faculty of Music, asking me to please come. Aiyana's searchlight eyes caught me the moment I walked in. She was seated in an office chair.

"We've been having a nice chat. But she can't sit here forever. Come back when summer is over, I keep telling her. I've been explaining that a pianist needs training before the playing can amount to anything. Like a voice needs training."

A defiant Aiyana sank deeper into her chair.

"I've been explaining that most people just play for their own pleasure, like most people sing, you know, for their own enjoyment."

Aiyana lips were set. She was not moving.

"Unless it's my singing we're talking about." Mrs. Bond smiled. "For other people's discomfort, flaps needed. You know, like those winter caps with the flaps that come down over your ears?"

I said, "Isn't there someone here who can listen to her play? That's all she's asking."

"I'm afraid there isn't."

"But she's a musical genius. A musical savant, like Leslie Lemke and Derek Paravicini."

"Are they students here?"

"No, of course not. They were born with a gift. They didn't need to take lessons in special schools. But they did need someone to hear them play."

"They must have been students somewhere."

Aiyana got up and retreated to the door. "I'm coming back tomorrow. And the next day. And the next day until someone listens to me play."

I said to Mrs. Bond, "See you tomorrow."

CHAPTER TWENTY

Eric

I awoke to another hot day with no AC. I eased open the bedroom door. Although it was ten past nine, Aiyana was still asleep in my bed, wrapped in Julia's blue blanket. She turned from her back to her side and curled up, knees to her chest, hands covering her face, and began to moan and cry out. When she turned again, flinging both arms over her head, I touched her shoulder to shake her awake. Her eyes blinked open, staring at me first in fear, then in confusion, then in recognition. Then, with a slight smile, she turned on her side and went back to sleep.

The bedroom smelled of Julia's apricot-and-apple shampoo. Mixed, they smelled like neither. Combined with Julia's blue blanket, Aiyana smelled and looked like both Aiyana and Julia. I waited at the door, hoping for another nightmare so I could wake her up again and touch her shoulder again so I could see that slight smile again.

I lay listening to Julia's grandfather clock in the corner by my bookcase. I could hear in the tick-tock of that old clock what Julia had called the infinity of time — that if you listen to it long enough, an old tick-tock clock will turn time into an infinity of now. It will give meaning to the passing-away never-to-return but always-coming-back in the numbers of time. Julia had passed away, supposedly never to return, but in that moment in my bedroom, when I smelled for only a moment in time that shampoo, there Julia was, no doubt about it, caught between the tick and the tock of time.

I checked the tick-tock time against the numbers on my watch. Nine thirty. I wished Aiyana would wake up so I could look at her sitting in the chair Julia had always sat in as I served her breakfast on this particular never-to-return tick-tock morning and accept the fact that by some twist of fate, Aiyana, a seventeen-year-old kid I had picked up off the street was now under Julia's blue blanket in the bed of a twenty-nine-year-old man. That was not normal. But nothing about this situation was normal.

I sat at the table and waited. Needing to do something while I waited, I went into the bathroom, straightened the towels, wiped the soap dish, and returned the toothpaste to its proper spot, which meant that Julia, a twenty-five-year-old woman who never tidied up, had been using my bathroom. I filled the basin with warm water to wash my face. When I pulled the plug, the water swept in a circle, gurgled, and too slowly, disappeared down the drain. Needed a little plumber. That meant that Aiyana, a seventeen-year-old kid, whose constant combing and brushing and fiddling with her hair was plugging the drain, was now using my bathroom.

I waited at the living-room window. I checked the cars parked along the street. I'd taken the time to learn which car belonged to which house. All the parking spots were arranged in order, so even if Hartley was not driving the Caddy, I would notice.

I went back to the bedroom. Aiyana was standing at the window, hugging the blanket. "He's got his bolt cutter. He's drunk and he's got his gun."

"I just checked. He's not out there."

Aiyana grabbed my arm and pulled me into the closet. We pushed in behind Julia's hanging coats and dresses. I felt fear in the grip of her fingers around my forearm, and in the trembling of her leg against mine. We stood wedged together in the darkness, unable to move. I felt useless, hiding in the closet. But her fear had immobilized me.

Footsteps thumped across the living room and entered the bedroom. A faint rustle of paper, the rasp of a match, and cigarette smoke filtered into the blackness. One by one, drawers rattled open and shut. Then footsteps crossed the room again, the headboard banged against the wall as he sat heavily on the bed and smoked his cigarette.

As we squeezed together between Julia's dresses, Aiyana's thigh against mine, her hair against my cheek, I felt the cold fingers of a hand creep up my back, pushing me against this girl now wearing Julia's blue blanket. I placed my hand over hers, careful not to touch the freshly healed fingers, and held it, and it stayed there in mine. But the pulse I felt beating against my wrist seemed not to be mine or hers, and I had the eerie sense that at any moment another hand might reach into the closet and take my hand, and I would not hear, *Where are you?* I would hear, *Here I am.*

More footsteps, this time approaching the closet. Hartley stood a few inches away, smoking, drawing in, breathing out. He seemed to be waiting for us to betray ourselves as we waited for him to open the closet door. Finally, as the muscles along the back of my legs began to ache with tension, Hartley's boots wandered off across the living room. I heard the door close.

Gradually, as the cigarette smoke was replaced by the scent of Julia's apple-and-apricot shampoo, I relaxed. Aiyana opened the door a crack. I let go of her hand and we stepped from the closet.

"He knows I'm here for sure now. He stole my lighter. I left it right there and now it's gone."

She sat on the bed. She held up a string of blue rosary beads. "These were in the pocket of Julia's coat hanging in the closet."

Now I had the feeling that the other hand I'd felt in the closet had followed me and was the hand holding Julia's rosary beads. I wanted to sit beside her and take that hand again but I was afraid that it would be the hand with the cold fingers.

"He stole my lighter," Aiyana repeated. "It was on the dresser."

Thankful for the change of topic, I said, "I'll get you another one."

"There is no other one."

She got up and wrapped Julia's blanket around herself and then headed into the living room where she sank into Julia's recliner. She began to curl one long strand of hair around her index finger.

I straightened the bedding and went into the living room and sat on the chesterfield. "This guy Hartley is a real prince. Is he like a permanent boyfriend?"

She removed the blanket. Her fingers checked along the line of buttons of the pyjamas, making certain each was done up. "Sometimes. They have fights and he disappears and then he comes back. That's what men do. They come. They drink. They smoke. They fight. They leave. And then, after a while, they come back. Is that George knocking on the door? Is that Frank knocking on the door?"

She folded both legs underneath her and leaned her head against the back of the recliner. Her body was slumped with fatigue, her face filled with anxiety. She began to slide the rosary beads through her fingers, chanting, "Is that Mike knocking on the door? Is that John knocking on the door?"

I said, "Is that Hartley knocking on the door?" I held a paper out to her. "I found this on the bed."

She looked at it. "I can't read, remember?"

Before I read it to her, I said, "Call Socks. She must be around here somewhere."

She called.

I waited for Socks to appear, to come over and rub against Aiyana's leg until she picked her up and settled her on her lap. When Socks did not appear, I read Aiyana the note: "Since you're in the closet anyway, pack your stuff. I've got Socks down in the Caddy waiting for you. If you're not packed and ready by ten o'clock, I'll break the cat's neck."

CHAPTER TWENTY-ONE

Aiyana

For my next trip to the university, I'd planned to put on one of the outfits Eric had bought for me, a sleeveless black top, distressed jeans, and black-strap sandals. I hadn't wanted anything hooters or bush bait — low cut, bare midriff, spaghetti straps, off the shoulder with no straps — the way almost all the girls dressed at the mall. Mall bait.

As though my thinking about hooters and bush bait had invited him here, when we opened the apartment door, there Hartley stood, Socks under one arm. One-handed, he took out his cigarettes, stuck one in his mouth, and lit a match.

"Give me the cat," Eric said.

Hartley shook out the match and sucked in the smoke. "Try taking it off me."

I knew he was drunk, and the bulge under his plaid shirt told me he had his gun tucked into his wide leather belt.

"I'll go with Hartley," I said. "That way no one gets hurt."

Eric's lips had tightened and I knew what was coming if I didn't grab my stuff. Hartley would wring Sock's neck and, with a smirk, give Eric the cat, just like he asked for.

I went into the bedroom and changed into jeans and a t-shirt. I picked up a change of clothes and my purse. I slipped on my new sandals and walked past Eric and out the door. He reached out as I passed him; he looked like he wanted to say something, but I shrugged him off and followed Hartley, Socks under one arm, down the hall. From the street, I glanced back at Eric watching at the window. I climbed into the Caddy.

We were halfway down the block before Hartley handed Socks over to me.

"So, sweetheart. You've come to your senses and you're coming home. Your mother is worried."

Hartley threw his cigarette butt out of the window and lit another from a package of Player's, and another, and all of a sudden we were on the 401. He took a bottle from under the seat and had a drink. He reached across my legs and opened the glove compartment for his sunglasses. As his arm drew back, his hand brushed against my thigh.

"Want a drink, sweetheart?"

We reached the 400 cut-off and continued north.

I could ask him to stop at the next restaurant to go to the washroom and then disappear out the back door. But that would mean leaving Socks. I could ask him to stop along the shoulder of the road so Socks could go and then I could disappear into the woods. But everywhere was empty fields with no woods to disappear into.

Now he was finishing his bottle of Canadian Club. Next he'd be asking me to throw the empty out the window. Next he'd be asking me to put on a George Jones CD. Next he'd be looking for a motel. I thought, next is not a round-and-round word. It's a go-forward word. It's a make-a-plan word.

He handed me the empty and opened another. The more he drank the faster he drove, the old Caddy passing every car in sight. So I was thankful when he turned into a gas station with a motel and restaurant. He shut off the engine and picked up the cat. "I'm gonna get us a room. If you run while I'm gone, I'll rip the cat's head off."

He went into the office and came out in a few minutes with a key.

"Let's go, sweetheart. Get some shut-eye."

"It's not shut-eye time. It's eat-dinner time."

"It's sleep time for me. I'm done for the day. Come in and have a drink with ol' Hartley. We can order something from the kitchen and then you can sleep wherever you want."

"Yeah, right. Have a little room service with ol' Hartley."

"Suit yourself. I've got the cat."

He got out of the car. He ambled up to the line of motel doors and unlocked room 5. The light snapped on. Through the open curtains I could see him moving around, removing his plaid shirt, pouring a drink, lighting a Player's.

I stretched my feet across the seat and closed my eyes. Even if I did leave Socks, which I never would, I had no idea how to get away, and no idea where to go. All these years and all these Hartleys should have taught me more tricks than Saturday-afternoon wrestling, the standard afternoon program of every double-wide boy in the Double-Wides Park, that is if they weren't feeling up bush bait in the ice huts.

The soreness from my wrist was gone, replaced by the soreness in my foot from the new-leather stiffness of the sandals. I folded my arms across my chest and rubbed my bare arms, for now, late afternoon, it was cooler. I put on two more t-shirts.

As time dragged on, I became so worried about Socks that I got out of the car and crept barefoot across the pavement to the motel. I opened the door and stood waiting until my eyes adjusted to the dark. I saw the bed in the centre of the room and the outline of Hartley under the blankets. I stepped inside. Overpowering the smell of cigarettes and alcohol, the familiar odour of Hartley's feet filled the room. From wearing those boots all the time, winter or summer. He wore those same socks winter and summer too, it smelled like. The cat was cleaner than Hartley. Socks washed her feet ten times a day.

I stepped inside and felt along the floor and behind the combination TV stand and dresser. No cat. I checked the bathroom. I checked under an old living-room chair and then dropped to the floor to look under the bed.

His arm snaked out and fastened around my wrist. "Couldn't resist, eh, sweetheart?"

He tried to pull me down beside him but I braced my knees on the edge of the bed. Leaning back to get leverage, my hand landed on one of his work boots. I swung it overhead, smashing Hartley across the forehead. He let go with a yelp and I stumbled back.

He rubbed his forehead but didn't get out of bed. "I got your cat under the covers. If you run your hand up between my legs you can give it a pat."

Hartley folded his arms across his chest and closed his eyes. I waited for his snoring to begin. It would soon be dark and it would soon be night and I would still be waiting and Hartley would still be sleeping.

In the coffin, my father had looked like someone sleeping. He was wearing one of the suits he wore to his office job at the paper mill, his arms folded across his chest. He'd disappeared through the ice in December and spent the rest of the winter frozen, and when I found him on the shoreline he was frozen stiff and still, and in the coffin he still looked frozen, so I thought, when he thaws out he'll come home for pork chops in mushroom soup.

Father Clark said, "Do you want to say anything to your father? I'll write it for you and we'll give it to him."

I said, "Dear Daddy. Don't be late for supper. We're having your favourite: pork chops in mushroom soup."

As Father Clark wrote the note, I wiped at my tears with his white handkerchief that had tiny crosses embroidered in each corner. I folded the note, and Father Clark and I went up to the coffin. Father Clark put the note under his hands that were folded together. I didn't need to touch them to know that they were cold.

I gave my father one last look. His hair was sandy brown. He was tall and lean. His face was tanned. His suit was one shade of blue with darker hidden blue flecks that came to life as he walked each morning from the door into the dawn that brought to life that same camouflaged energy of hidden blues as in the underwater currents that had brought him to me on the shoreline.

And now, strangely, like looking down at Hartley from the sky, I could see him floating in the different shades of blue with bluer flecks in the centre of the underwater currents. And now looking down, I could see in the pine trees all around him the different shades and layers of green turning greener as they came to life in the sun.

But there was no sun in the church that day and no sun outside either and there was no sun in this motel room. But the day Eric pulled up in his Wrangler on Madison Avenue and got out, there was sun, and he was wearing a blue sports jacket with darker flecks of blue in the sun. So from that moment on, I expected something from Eric. But I couldn't tell what that something was or why I felt it, for the energy that was all around him seemed hidden by the filmy shadow of the black lace of someone else's energy.

If only my eyes had been able then to see the energy I saw now, how different everything would be. Julia should be gone. I'd left her at the bottom of the lake. And that was why she was back here now. And now she'd put this string of rosary beads into my hand, each one a tiny blue marble filled with spots of blue with darker flecks of blue in the sun.

It would soon be dark and it would soon be night and then it will be tomorrow and I will be suspended between here and there by this one thin wire running bead to bead from me to her like I was her life-support machine with blinking lights beating a mechanical pulse from me to her, bead to bead, punishment for trying to get rid of her by leaving her in that senseless piece of junk at the frozen bottom of that frigid lake.

CHAPTER TWENTY-TWO

Eric

Dust floated in a bar of late-evening sunlight slanting through the window onto my living-room floor. Aiyana had cleaned the apartment two days ago and now it was time again, probably from needing the windows open at night to cool things off. When I heard the outer door open, I got up, convinced I would find Aiyana and Socks in the hall. But it was the lock-repair company.

I packed a few things in my gym bag and set off, up Avenue Road to the 401 and then to the 400. Dropping down to the steel bridge that I remembered from the last trip, I saw the laneway with a sign for Broken Deer Double-Wides. According to Google, trailer 27B was a right turn, first lot on the left, a brown aluminum-clad trailer with a wood-framed side porch. The lots on either side were empty, so I pulled in beside the Caddy. The entire trailer park seemed deserted, the double-wides that remained were boarded up, no cars anywhere. But I noticed at the end of a path to the lake several outboards were docked. Left there, I guessed, to be picked up later.

I shut off the Wrangler. Before I could ease my cramped legs into standing, the side door of the trailer swung open and a woman dressed in a rumpled plaid shirt and sagging brown slacks appeared on the porch.

A bottle of beer in one hand and a cigarette in the other, she blinked against the late-afternoon sun as though she'd just gotten out of bed.

"Who are you looking for?"

"Aiyana."

"Aiyana," the woman called over her shoulder. "There's someone here. Can I invite him in for a beer?"

From inside I heard Aiyana answer, "No, Mother. He doesn't want a beer."

But her mother waved for me. "Come in for a beer."

One look at this sagging mother in this neglected trailer in this desolate trailer park convinced me I was not going to leave without Aiyana. I followed a path through the weeds and twitch grass to the porch steps. I opened the screen door and stepped in. At one time, living a better life somewhere else, her mother might have been attractive. But now, overweight, eyes glazed from drink, she belonged where she was, in this smoke-yellowed kitchen with the counter and sink filled with dirty glasses and the table cluttered with empty beer bottles and crusted plates.

To my left, one door led into a dingy bedroom; to my right, another door led into an equally dingy living room; and through a doorway straight ahead, I assumed were two more bedrooms, although that side of the double-wide seemed dark and empty.

Aiyana was angry, her eyes flashing. "You shouldn't be here. What are you doing here?"

Her mother, slumped at the kitchen table, dragged on her cigarette. Her eyebrows furrowed, she seemed to be trying to figure out who I was and what was going on.

Aiyana pulled up a chair opposite her mother. "Mona, this is Eric, a friend from Toronto."

Mona looked confused, like a kid waiting to be told what to do next. It seemed obvious that Aiyana was her mother's caregiver, probably had been since Aiyana was a child.

Mona emptied her beer. She held her fist over her mouth for a quiet burp. "Does yer frien' wanna beer?"

Leaning against the kitchen counter, contemplating mother and daughter, I shook my head. Mona got up and opened the fridge. "Do you wanna beer, Hartley?"

"Sure as hell do," replied a gravelly voice from the bedroom.

"How about yer frien'? Does he wanna beer?"

"His name is Eric Cooper."

Mona looked at me from a watery distance. "Do you wan—"

Hartley appeared. He picked up his baseball hat from the top of the refrigerator and stuck it on the back of his half-bald head. As he approached the table, tucking in his shirt, I noticed the silver studs along his belt, which was wide and black with a silver cowboy buckle.

"I'm sure you remember Eric Cooper," said Aiyana.

Hartley swung his arm forward. "Put 'er in the vice, Coop." The long thin fingers of the calloused hand collapsed mine into a claw. He slurred through the cigarette dangling from his lips, "How ya doin', Cooper?" He tipped his hat forward and looked down his nose at me before releasing my numbed hand. He sat at the table and hooked one long leg over the other. "What brings you here?" His breath reeked of alcohol.

"I was just passing by," I said.

Aiyana eyed me quizzically.

"Passing by. Ha! That's a good one. This road don't go no place. White Crow Falls, but that's no place."

"I've just dropped in to see Aiyana." I glanced around. "I wanted to have a look, check the place out."

Hartley dragged on his cigarette. "So what do you think, now that you've had a look and checked the place it out? Ready to leave, I bet."

"What I think, now that I've had a look and checked the place out, is that this is a filthy trailer with a drunk mother with a drunk boyfriend, which is not a suitable place for Aiyana to be staying, especially considering the stink you're now making by butting your cigarette on a crusted dinner plate. So, yeah, I think Aiyana and I are ready to leave."

Mona looked up. A glimmer of intelligence crossed her face. "I know, I know. I know the place is a mess. But I ain't had time to clean up, between one thing and th'other, been too busy."

"Too busy!" exploded Hartley. "Ha! He's right. Too drunk, you mean. But you nailed it, Coop. These old double-wides are like living in a place with dog hair. Don't matter how much you clean up, you'll always find more." He drilled his little finger into his ear, studied the excavated debris, and wiped it on his pants. "It's so filthy in here you gotta wipe yer feet on the way out. So if I was you, Coop. I'd be right now wiping my feet on the way out."

Mona straightened up, her eyes glassy but awake. "Why should I clean up? Ain't no one here to clean it up for."

"Not even for me?" Aiyana suggested.

Mona heaved herself upright to standing. She emptied the smoking dinner plate into the heavy black frying pan sitting in the sink. The butt sizzled in the layer of stale grease. "I get lonely, you know, all by myself, all day long. Why don't you at least come for a visit?"

"Yeah right. Mother and daughter, shotgun a few beers, talk about old times, crunch a few cold ones." Aiyana slid her chair back and went outside, slamming the screen door, leaving me alone with Mona and Hartley.

"What's the matter with her?" Mona wondered. "Just 'cause I had a few beers? What's the matter with that? Hartley, what's the matter with that?"

Hartley drained his glass. "What's the matter with that is I just finished my beer. Get me another one." He shifted his chair away from the table and undid his belt. He took a rag and a bottle of metal cleaner from the drawer in the table and began to polish the silver buckle.

"What's the matter with having a few beers?" Mona asked emptily. "How would she feel all alone here all day with no one to talk to?" She turned to me. "I had to raise her all by myself. All I had to live on was my gov'ment cheque, twenty-two hundred an' eighty-five dollars. I couldn't afford no piana. That's all she ever wanted. Her own piana. And then, two weeks ago, three weeks ago maybe, she left, walked out one day and disappeared. I can see her now, just got up from the table and walked across the kitchen and out the door, just like she did now. Didn't even take any clothes. I was sittin' right here, well not right here, in that chair there, just like I am now and — wasn't I, Hartley — and she—"

"Yup, down to Toronto to work as a stripper. Her and that old cat. Me and Jimmy George used to take old cats fishing for old ladies. We'd put them in a mesh onion bag with a stone on the bottom, ten bucks a cat."

The polished buckle gleamed in the grimy light coming through the grimy window. Hartley refastened his belt and opened the drawer again and took out what looked like an old-fashioned cowboy six-shooter. He began to polish the handle.

"'Baby,' I says, 'where you goin'?' 'I'm leaving,' she says, and out the door she goes. And the next day, I got a letter from the gov'ment saying they're gonna cut her off. How did they know she was gone when she'd only just left?"

"They cut her off because she was turnin' eighteen. Shut the fuck up about it and get us another beer."

Mona crossed the cracked linoleum to the refrigerator for two more beers.

Hartley sighted down the barrel at me. "The government watches her on the internet to figure out ways to cut her off. They got them little drones that look like bugs that fly around with them little cameras, takin' pictures of what she's doin' with the money they send her."

Finished polishing his six-shooter, Hartley stuck it in his belt. He got up and opened a closet and brought out a rifle. "This is an old Lever-Action .22 I bought at the auctions. Ever used one of these, Coop? They'll tell you it's a farm gun, not powerful enough to kill anybody. But a shot through the head at three hundred yards will drop you dead in the farm yard."

He sat at the table and poured some Lucas Gun Metal Polish onto his rag. He said, "Mona, put on some music and liven the place up a little. One of them Hank Snow LPs."

"You just played Hank Snow. Play Ray Price."

"I don't want fuckin' Ray Price. I want fuckin' Hank Snow."

Mona disappeared into the living room.

Hank Snow began and Hartley began to tap on the floor with one boot. Then he began to sing along with Hank Snow's "Lonesome Blue Yodel," beating time to the tune with the nod of his head. When Mona reappeared, he set the .22 aside, got up, and pulled her to the centre of the kitchen. Because he was tall and she was short, he danced bent over in angles as they careened across the room and banged against the opposite wall. Hank Snow jumped from his groove and the music stopped. Mona disappeared into the living room. Hank Snow returned.

"Come on, sweetheart," he said to Aiyana when she reappeared in the kitchen doorway. "Let's us have a dance."

He grabbed her and dragged her to the centre of the room. When Hartley crashed against the kitchen counter, she slipped out of his grip. But Hartley grabbed her again and resumed the dance, whirling across the floor and into the living room and back. In her struggle to twist out of his arms, Aiyana tripped and fell to her knees at my feet. When Hartley tried to pull her upright, I stopped him. "She doesn't want to dance."

Hartley teetered a little before regaining his balance and squaring his lanky frame. Head tilted back, eyes narrowed, he asked, "What's up your nose, ol' buddy?"

"She doesn't want to dance." I was not worried about fighting a too-drunk-to-stand-up drunk. But I was concerned about the guns.

Hartley hooked his thumbs into his freshly polished belt. "She doesn't want to dance. Oh indeed. Golly jeepers. With all due disrespect, I don't think it's any of your fuckin' business."

Mona appeared. "Don't get her upset, Hartley. I told you. She'll have a meltdown." Mona wrapped her arms around Hartley's neck and they resumed the dance.

"You watch it, Coop. You watch your mouth." Hartley lurched into the music and across the kitchen they went, stepping so heavily that the dishes on the counter rattled. But when he slammed into the kitchen table, Mona fell sideways, knocking me backward onto the floor. I felt a jolt in my shoulder as I got up. Aiyana took my arm and led me outside.

She sat on the porch step and began her hair obsession, curling one long strand around her finger, then picking up another. I sat beside her and rubbed my shoulder and watched her. She let this piece go and collected another and drew it across her cheek like a black ribbon.

I took her hand. "We're going. You can't stay here."

"Yeah, I guess. But I'm used to it. He gets drunk, he gets, you know, macho. He keeps the revolver in a drawer, except when he gets really drunk and he brings it out and, you know, struts around."

"Aiyana. Hear what I'm saying. We have to leave."

She picked up another strand and twisted it around her finger and dropped it and picked up another. I couldn't understand why she wasn't crying or attacking somebody. "This is craziness. How do you put up with this? How can you live like this?"

She was quiet, worrying her hair, staring at the patch of bare ground below the first step. When she raised the good hand to her mouth and began to bite at the nail of the index finger. I took her hand. "Stop it. See what this place does to you?"

She put the hand into her pocket and pulled out the rosary beads and began to slide them one at a time, staring at each one. "If I go back with you, he'll come after me."

"I'll get an apartment where he can't find you."

The screen door slammed behind us. Hartley fished a pack of Player's from the pocket of the plaid shirt, which was open, showing a skull-and-crossbones heavy-metal tattoo on his chest. "You ever heard of dead silence, Coop? Because dead silence is going to be what you'll be hearing if you don't get into your Wrangler and leave."

Aiyana got up. "He's leaving in a few minutes. I want to show him the lake and then he leaves."

I followed her criss-cross through the unoccupied double-wides, no sign of life anywhere. Aiyana explained, "The gravel boss said she can stay here for free until the bulldozers come as long as there's no trouble."

As we got closer to the water, the late-afternoon sun brightened our path away from the trailer and past a canoe next to two upside-down aluminum row boats. We walked across a patch of sand and sat on a log at the shore's edge. Before us the water glinted in silvery ripples on the glassy surface.

She said, "Mrs. Battler used to swim down here. There used to be bullrushes growing along here. On hot days, if there wasn't anyone around, she'd just strip and go in. She used to swim from here to Devil's Island. My Grampa Willie warned her about the current, but she didn't listen. She disappeared one summer day. They found her in the spring, washed up in the ice, at the end of the lake."

Because of the glare off the water, I couldn't see Aiyana's face and couldn't guess why she had brought me here, but I could tell, I had gotten to know her well enough, that she was about to open up about something so I waited.

She pointed to the far side of the lake. "A man who worked for the railroad had a cottage over there. He had this shoe-polish black comb-over hairdo where he brought the long strings up from the back of his head and held them in place with glue. It was good glue because even on a windy day the hairdo stayed in place. The boys used to steal his leaky rowboat and come all the way over here to drink beer. I don't know why because they could just as easily have drunk beer over there. Just the idea of stealing a boat, I guess. Six guys and a case of beer in a rowboat."

She shifted on the log and wrapped her arms around her knees. "Then one day they left a note: Why don't you use some of that hair glue to fix the leaks in your rowboat? So the railroad man put a lock on the boat so they couldn't steal it anymore. But not long after that, one of the guys bought an old car, so then it was six guys and a case of beer in an old car."

"Then, not long after that, the railroad man went fishing and his leaky boat sunk and the current took him to the far end of the lake and they found him in the spring when the ice came out."

She picked up a stone at her feet, no colours, grey like the gravel pits that were all over the place. Although, I thought, just because I couldn't see the colours, it didn't mean she couldn't.

"Then those six guys got six girls pregnant, and it was six guys and a case of beer in someone's leaky double-wide. Soon those six babies will grow up to be six kids and a case of beer in a stolen rowboat. Round and round we go, spokes in the wheel, one stage to the next." She got up. "I want to see if Uncle Jimmy's skiff is here."

I followed her along the lane to a path through the trees to the other side of the dock. Another canoe with paddles was right side up on the shore, and the skiff was upside down a few feet from the dock. We sat on the skiff. About one hundred yards off the cove stood a dead tree that looked like it was split in half by lightning. She pointed toward it. "My dad caught a fifteen-pound largemouth there once, right across from that tree. He left it tied overnight in the water at the end of the dock and the snapping turtles ate it."

I couldn't resist. Now that that she was talking about her childhood, I wanted a better look. "I'm trying to understand a seventeen-year-old teenager, yes, but unlike any teenager I've ever met. Tell me more about yourself, growing up. And the priest. How am I to understand the priest?"

Aiyana nodded. "Yeah. I know what you might think, but no, Father Clark was a good priest, trying to help me. He discovered me the day after his piano arrived. They told him the church had no piano so he had one shipped up from Toronto. I watched them unload it and then after they were gone, I sat down and played it. This scruffy little trailer-park kid. He couldn't believe what he was hearing." She smiled a little. "His word for me was *enhanced*. But I didn't think so. All I ever wanted was to be an ordinary kid."

"Then what? With you and Father Clark."

"Yeah, I know what you want to hear." She reached down for two blades of grass. "Have you ever tried the soft part? It's sweet. Try it."

She nibbled at the white end. I waited.

"I don't know if you've ever met a person like Father Clark. If you had, then you would know, when such a person stands before you — whether you've ever seen such a person before or heard of such a person before or believed that such a person could even exist — you'd know that person is special because that person's eyes are full of something you want to have, and you won't know what that something is, but you will know it comes from a place you'd like to be, and you'd know wherever that was, it was on the other side."

"Aiyana. What other side? Why do you keep saying that?"

She pulled up a longer blade of grass and began to chew on the white end. "In the winter my dad always wore a green parka, kind of like watermelon colour, so he wasn't easy to see in the dark, but in the daylight, like right now, I could see him crossing the ice from the other side."

"Aiyana, what other side?"

"It's like looking at what's happening in the bubble we live in but the important stuff is happening outside the bubble. Father Clark told me his first church was in an old building with an old boiler furnace that had reducing valves to control the water pressure. The mind is like that, he said. It acts as a reducing valve that protects us from knowing more than we can handle and understand. But in those moments before death, as the brain shuts down, the valve opens up, and all we need to know about this side and the other side rushes into our mind, like the rushing of water into an old boiler furnace."

She drew a long breath and gave a long sigh. "Father Clark always had a package of mints in his pocket for when he was explaining stuff to me, and he always gave me one and took one for himself, and he'd suck on his mint for a minute and I'd suck on my mint for a minute, and then he'd say, 'Have I told you the minnow story' and I would say no, even though he had, because I wanted another mint. 'Well,' he would say, 'from the bottom of the pond, the minnows with big staring eyes could look up through the ripples and watch the water striders skating across the blue above, wondering what was beyond that ceiling and wondering what was the meaning of the words being written by those thready legs overhead. So the minnows formed study groups and put together research committees to find a way to go from this side of the water ceiling to the other side, so they could ask the water striders this question: How did you get from this side to the other side?

"'But the minnows couldn't find a way to get beyond the blue ceiling of the water, and no matter how far they swam looking up with those big blinkless telescope eyes, even if they swam on and on looking up, there was no end to the water and there was no end to the ceiling of water and there was no one among anyone able to swim through the ceiling of water and find out what was beyond, on the other side.'

"Then he would give me another mint.

"'So the minnows decided there wasn't anything beyond the blue ceiling of water, and anyone who thought otherwise was hallucinating — all but this very little minnow called Aiyana who knew that on this side of the ceiling of water, in this place that the minnows called the pond, that the minnows were already drinking from the water the information they were looking for. The words of the teachings they were looking for were in their mouths already, for the answers were not beyond the ceiling of the water, but in the water itself.'"

I drew a long breath and I gave a long sigh. By now I had a headache. At least my head thought I had a headache. I wasn't sure what my head thought or not thought. "Okay. A nice story. But I'm not a poet. I'm a mathematician."

"Okay. You're a mathematician." Aiyana pulled up three long blades of grass and laid them on the boat's bottom surface. "What is that?"

"A triangle."

She tossed them aside. "Now that triangle is gone. But if there were no more triangles, and no people to see a triangle, the triangle would still exist, so where would it be?"

"I get it. The theorem of Pythagoras existed before Pythagoras brought it into existence. So what?"

"Where did it exist?"

This was getting annoying. "I don't know. Aiyana."

"You do know. Think of numbers in mathematical equations like notes in music. If there were no fingers to play the notes of Chopin's Polonaise, and no ears to hear the music, would the pattern or the blueprint for the notes and the music of Chopin's Polonaise still be there, waiting for someone to put the notes together into that pattern and play them?"

"Make them real you mean?"

"They're already real. The pattern is what's real because the pattern is permanent. The copies of the patterns are impermanent, here today gone tomorrow. The combination of notes coming from the piano to make a song are simply copies of the pattern. The pattern of notes for Chopin's Hungarian Rhapsody existed before Chopin wrote them down and before anyone played them. All the music there is, all the music that will ever be is there, even if there's no one to play it or no one to hear it. All you need is for someone to play the notes in that particular pattern."

I thought, well, this sort of makes sense, except one problem: "Where is the pattern? And don't say on the other side. Because that is the problem. Because I'll still have the feeling there's something wrong with this theory, but I can't put my finger on it."

"Father Clark would hold up his finger. He'd say, 'Ah, Eric, my boy. Exactly. You can't put your finger on it. You can't hold it in your hand. It's like a shadow. It's there but you can't pick it up.'"

"So okay. But what's the point?"

"The point, Eric my boy, is the point."

"So where is the other side?"

"On the other side of the bubble you're living in. On the other side of the frame you're living in. On the other side of the current you're floating in."

She threw the stone overhand. I watched it drop with a hollow plunk into the water, the concentric circles spreading across the surface.

She said, "I come here because straight out, about a hundred yards out, is where my father drowned. If you drown here, the current will take you thirty feet under, and you'll drift toward the channel. Pick up a stick, cut a notch in it, throw in the stick, watch it disappear. Six months from now, it'll surface at the other end."

She closed her eyes and placed her good hand palm down on her thigh, like closing a book, like setting it down on a table, having read me the words of the last sentence. I could not see her face and was trying to guess what she might be thinking when she said, "I can hear the swish of the current. Can you hear it?"

I listened. I could hear the distant rush of something, in the stillness fading away and receding and then rising up again in waves before growing weak and distant. I seemed to be hearing it in layers, a sound I might normally hear, but this one overlaid with other different sounds, altering the exactitude of what she thought I heard, which meant that what I thought was the exact sound, maybe was not.

"It's like an echo, Eric. It's like a shadow, Eric."

Maybe I could hear in that distant swish-swish of a current, maybe something in how I heard it passed between it and me because I had the sense that I had put my finger on it, even though I couldn't quite put my finger on it.

I said, "But you can't quite put your finger on it."

"You don't need to put your finger on it to know it's there."

CHAPTER TWENTY-THREE

Eric

We retraced our footsteps up the path, me beside her, slow steps through the grass and along a gravel path. Twice her arm touched mine as we crossed the yard and mounted the porch steps. I opened the screen door for her and we stepped inside.

She paused a moment to listen. "They're passed out."

As she slipped past, she brushed my shoulder, making me flinch.

"Ouch," she apologized. "The shoulder."

"It's all right, just sore from the walk."

"I'll rub it with Absorbine."

I sat at the table and she poured the liniment. As her hand rubbed across my shoulder, the gold necklace swinging gently, the pulse in her neck beat softly with the movement of her body. She stood close, leaning over me. She leaned closer, her cheek close to mine, her lips close to my ear. I waited for her to whisper something. But when I heard it, I could not believe it: "Hartley is planning to put a rock in an onion bag and drown Socks if you don't leave."

She returned the cap to the bottle and went to the sink to wash her hand. She went through the door into the other side of the trailer.

She was gone and I was alone, lost at the kitchen table, listening to her footsteps, crossing back and forth, on the other side.

The door into the other side stood ajar. With the tips of my fingers, I pushed it all the way open. I felt along the wall but could find no light switch. As my eyes adjusted to the gloom, into focus came a doorway to the left or maybe it was a doorway to the right. I wasn't sure. I thought through one of these doorways I would find … I didn't know what … maybe on a little table I would find a picture of her sitting on the cabin step, or a picture of her holding up a fish she'd caught with her dad, or a picture of her setting up a tent with Grandpa Willie. But no, as I got closer, what I saw was a picture of her framed in some other doorway, her arm partly raised to say goodbye, or partly raised to say hello, I couldn't tell which.

I had known her only a handful of days, but I'd learned to read her thoughts and feelings, as though I'd known her forever. I could picture in detail the exact way she walked. I could see in exact detail those long legs striding up the sidewalk toward me, arms a little turned out, like a dancer. But more importantly, even things about her I'd not seen, it seemed I could see them too. Like the gesture of moving her hair from her face to tuck behind one ear. I couldn't recall seeing her doing that. Yet it seemed to be part of the album of pictures of Aiyana I now had in my memory, but I couldn't put my finger on them.

Another picture of Aiyana came to mind: Her gold necklace glinting in the sun along the back of her neck. Yes, I'd seen that. But I don't recall ever seeing the faint rays of light filtering through a stained-glass window in long pale bars of red and gold to settle on that gold necklace as she knelt at the altar of some church. Now I could see that clearly and I could see that it was the Broken Deer church, although I'd never been in the Broken Deer Church and never seen her kneeling in any church. But I could see this picture as clearly as if I'd been an altar boy in this church. But I couldn't put my finger on it.

Hartley, a beer in each hand hanging from each gangly arm hanging from an unbuttoned plaid shirt, lurched down the porch steps and across the yard toward the Caddy. We watched him open the trunk and take out another case of Moosehead. Aiyana said to Mona who was at the screen door dressed in housecoat and slippers, "Mother, you've been drinking since seven a.m. Don't you think you've had enough?"

"What enough? What d'you mean. Enough what?"

"Enough what do you think?"

"Ah, baby, don't start arguments. Please. Don't give me one of your tongue lashings. That's what she does, what's-his-name, she gives me tongue lashings. She can't read or write but she can rip you apart with her tongue."

Hartley lurched past us and into the kitchen and slammed the beer case on the floor. "The queen came up here one time. Oh, indeed, to give everyone a tongue lashing about not taking advantage of opportunity. With Princess Diana. A tongue lashing. Oh, indeed. Wouldn't you enjoy that, Coop? A tongue lashing from Princess Aiyana?"

Mona rinsed two glasses in the sink and dried them on her sleeve. "Don' get upset, Aiyana. We're just havin' some fun. Hartley and I's jus' havin' a little fun. It's no fun aroun' here no more. It used to be fun, didn't it, Hartley? Remember? Didn't it used to be fun?"

"Golly jeepers, old chap — that's how the king talked."

Aiyana said, "That was Prince Phillip."

"Put on the music, Mona. Time to party." Hartley ripped open the top. "You guys wanna beer? Help yourself, Hartley. Don't mind if I do, Hartley, old chap. That's how he talked. Open me one too, Hartley, old chap. Then you and me can get a royal tongue lashing from Princess Aiyana."

Aiyana nudged me in warning: Forget it, Eric.

"Just kiddin', ol' buddy." Hartley sat on the beer case. He struck a match and lit a cigarette. "Live everyday like it's the last, that's my motto, ol' buddy."

Waving the Moosehead in time with the music he began to sing along with George Jones's, "He Stopped Loving Her Today."

I stared at this singing apparition, the narrow face and long neck bobbing back and forth in time with the music. Mona in a nasal monotone joined in — all three of them, George Jones, Mona, and Hartley — while beside me Aiyana waved her arms at the smoke, as round and round I was going in the impossibility of me surviving this day or any other day in this double-wide hell.

Hartley picked up the two-four of Moosehead. But partway to the refrigerator the case slipped from his arms and fell with a crash. Hartley stared at the crumpled box of smashed bottles.

"For Christ's sake," he muttered, folding himself down on his heels. "For fuck sakes," he mumbled, opening the top. Hartley began to pull out the broken necks. Mona found a plastic bag and a rag. Together they knelt by the case to retrieve with sober religious care each unbroken bottle, working together side by side, Hartley lifting the undamaged to the light while Mona wiped the saved clean. When they finished, they placed each bottle in the refrigerator, leaving the smashed on the floor.

God help me. I stood in the doorway and watched Hartley kneel at the refrigerator to slide onto the shelf each remaining Moosehead before grasping the handle and folding upward. He pulled himself into a bent-at-the-waist pry off; the resulting fizzing cap landed in the frying-pan grease. Hartley poured a beer and Mona poured a beer and they sat at the table with the resulting glasses of foam.

Hartley waved his pack of Player's. "Smoke, Hartley? Don't mind if I do, old chap." He fished in his shirt pockets. "Where's a match? You got a match, Hartley? Never mind, never mind, old chap, I got some in my two-hundred-horse royal carriage."

As he lurched through the puddle of beer, his shirttail, which was hanging down around the seat of his pants, snagged on the handle of the drawer by the sink. "Oops! I ripped my shirt. Holy shit, ripped my fuckin' shirt. Mona, get out here and fix my shirt. Mona, where the fuck are you?"

"I'm in here, Hartley. I'll be there…" Mona's nasal whine was drowned out by the flush of the toilet.

"Get out here and fix my shirt."

"In a minute, Hartley."

But not waiting, he undid his studded belt, tucked in the torn shirttail, and disappeared outside.

Aiyana began to pick up the glass and the soaked cardboard. Mona, now wearing tight black pants and a tight red sweater, emerged from the bathroom. The scent of perfume filled the kitchen. She blinked from beneath a layer of knock-off Dior. "Where's Hartley gone?"

"I think to the car for matches," I said.

"We got matches right here in the cupboard. What'd he go out there for?"

Hartley burst into the kitchen. "Who's for whisky?" He waved the bottle. "Golly jeepers, don't mind if I do, Hartley."

Aiyana crossed the kitchen and dumped the broken bottles into a bag under the sink and mopped the floor with a rag. I gathered up the cardboard and slipped it behind the refrigerator.

Hartley sat with his whisky, watching her. He scratched a match on the fly of his pants and lit a cigarette. He reached out to nudge Aiyana's leg as she passed. "I was at the movies once. I seen this adventure movie with Harrison Ford. He got shipwrecked on a desert island with a princess."

"It wasn't a shipwreck," said Aiyana. "It was an airplane crash."

He gulped down half his beer and then said to me, "Ol' buddy. How'd you like to get shipwrecked on a desert island with Princess Aiyana. Ain't she a sweetheart?"

"It was an airplane," Aiyana repeated.

Mona was nodding off, her arms folded across the tabletop.

"You could build yourself a hut outta bamboo fishing poles, lay yerself down on one of them bamboo mats, and get a tongue lashing."

"It would have to be a double-wide," said Aiyana.

"She could be your live-in bush bait. She could spear you fish with a pointed stick. You ever seen her gut a fish? Up here they have fish-guttin' contests, like who can do the Rubik's Cube the quickest. You ever go fishing, Coop? There's good fishing off Devil's Island. One of those islands with the palm trees. And sandy beaches, you and her naked on the sandy seaside, coconut trees and bananas and fish to gut and fry and a little hut built out of bamboo fishing poles, just you and the princess, hand hot as a pistol in your beachside pants giving you a hand lashing."

Hartley hoisted one leg and rested his beer-dripping work-booted foot on the tabletop. He studied the wet marks on the toe, wetted the fingers of his right hand with spit, and wiped at the beer. "Mona, wake up and get me a rag. And a pink grapefruit. She'd wear a grass skirt and flowers in her hair, like them Hawaiian girls, and have a basket of bananas on her head, ocean breeze blowing and her cooking fresh-gut fish over the open flames."

Hartley rubbed the beer off his boot with his shirt sleeve. He settled back in his chair and stared at Aiyana. "You and me, Aiyana, but not you, ol' buddy Coop. I sit by the campfire on Devil's Island drinkin' beer while the princess guts my fresh-caught fish and Coop goes back home wipe yer feet on the way out."

Hartley dragged to the end of his cigarette and butted it in the ashtray. He began to cough, a low guttural hacking so severe he had to rush to the bathroom to spit into the toilet. When he'd recovered, he unzipped his fly and began to urinate. Halfway through, realizing the door was open, he reached out and gave it a shove, slamming it shut.

I slid back my chair and stood. I motioned toward Aiyana, finger pointing, and mouthed the word *leave*. But she went through the door into the other side of the double-wide, to be alone, I assumed. I went into the living room and sat on the chesterfield, which seemed less shabby than the two faded blue chairs, and waited for Aiyana. When she didn't return, I found her on the other side curled up on the floor of the empty bedroom, her vacant eyes staring at nothing.

I lay beside her on the floor and waited for her to decide what to do next. I noticed the room was wallpapered with pictures of ducks. The yellowed window blind was hanging lopsided off the frame. On the other side of the wall would be the 1970s harvest-gold refrigerator, the sink filled with glasses, the counter strewn with dishes, and the table at which Hartley and Mona now sat playing blackjack, getting up from time to time for another Moosehead.

I lay beside her on the floor and waited. At about eight o'clock, Mona said she was tired of cards and was going to bed. I heard the bathroom door shut. I heard Hartley set down his glass and get up from the table and begin to put himself together: unbuckling his studded belt and opening his pants and tucking in his t-shirt and buttoning his plaid shirt and then sailing his baseball hat across the room to land on the refrigerator.

I lay on the floor beside Aiyana until, after a while, I heard the refrigerator door open. Hartley cleared his throat as he took out a beer and shut the door. I heard him cross the kitchen, pull up a chair, and sit at the table. I heard the scrape and fizzle of a match and the intake of breath. I smelled the acrid odour of a Player's.

Aiyana got up and disappeared into the other bedroom and returned dressed in a white bathrobe. She went along the hall and into the kitchen. She opened the refrigerator. I could hear her searching for something. She slammed the refrigerator door. "Stop staring."

"Just admiring the scenery."

I got up. I stood in the doorway of this side and watched. Holding her bathrobe tightly around herself, she drank a glass of milk, set the glass on the counter, and went into the bathroom. When the water began to run into the tub, Hartley got up. He listened at the door, then crept across the kitchen and disappeared outside. I hurried to the back porch in time to see Hartley going around the corner of the double-wide. I followed, wading through twitch grass as high as my knees. Hartley skirted a clump of bushes and crept along the wall to the bathroom window where, through partly drawn curtains he could see, as could I, Aiyana standing by the tub, waiting for the water to rise. I stepped forward, my stride slap-slapping through the grass, my arms swinging, ready to bang Hartley's moronic head against the siding.

He turned to face me. Shoulders back, hat slanted low, left thumb hooked in his belt, he said, "Step outside, Cooper."

"We are outside."

Hartley squared his shoulders. He adjusted his hat. He pulled out his Player's and stuck one in his mouth and lit the match and inhaled the smoke. Right eye squinting against the line of smoke ribboning from the cigarette, he looked down his nose at me. "All right then, ol' buddy. But you better watch your mouth."

He swaggered back to the porch.

I wasn't sure if he'd come back, so I sat in the grass below the window and listened to the water splashing into the tub. I felt the chill of the clear, cool evening air. I saw the shifting shades of moonlight reflecting blue and white on the water of the lake. I saw the silent shapes of green and brown moving in the trees, and the silver glints of moonlight dancing in the grass.

I got to my feet. As I turned I caught sight through the steamed-over bathroom window of a young woman sitting naked on the edge of the tub. Light from the ceiling fixture glinted on the gold chain around her bare neck. I knew that gold chain had belonged first to Julia and then to Aiyana but that gold chain on that naked woman did not seem to belong to Aiyana or to Julia.

I watched her run the fingers of one hand along her palm, gently prodding here and there, massaging the joints of each finger. I wanted to go through the wall and turn over that hand and read the palm to see who this woman was. I wanted to reach down and pick up the other hand and compare the two to see which of the two this woman had become. This line here, I would say as I gently rubbed my finger back and forth across the palm, this line here, which ends abruptly, I do not recognize as belonging to Julia's hand. And this line here is heavier, with a long stretch of unhappiness here, but a little later, a good heart line, I do not recognize as Aiyana's. So who is this?

I stroked the palm, the wrist, and the outer edge of each hand. I traced the tip of my finger across each hand, following the lines that would take me to the pulse that I would recognize as belonging to the one or to the other. I saw how the palm of one was different from the palm of the other, and I felt how the heart of the one was different from the heart of the other. I traced the tips of the fingers back to the wrist and felt how the wrist of the one was different from the wrist of the other.

When she stepped from the tub and stood to dry herself I stepped away from the window.

CHAPTER TWENTY-FOUR

Eric

I stepped back from the steamed over window and sank into the grass and leaned against the wall of the double-wide. I listened to the water drain from the tub. I heard the cabinet door snap open. I listened to the water running into the sink. I listened to her cleaning her teeth. I heard the toothbrush drop into the plastic holder. I heard the cabinet snap shut and I heard the gurgle of the drain in the gurgle in the pipes. I heard her leave the bathroom, shutting the door behind her.

How should I say goodbye on this our final day. Certainly, it could not be a bye-bye, see you later, drop me a line, have a nice trip. That would be like the goodbye you would say to a Hartley as he slipped into the water that would sink him to the bottom where the current would float him to the end of its run and wait there until he melted in spring. I had that picture in my mind when I was coming at him at the bathroom window. But of course, yes it was a picture in my mind, but I could not put my finger on it. But of course, yes, it was a feeling in my heart, but of course I could not put my finger on it.

Cremation was where I had gone wrong. That was my mistake. First I should have phoned my mom and dad who would have flown up from Boston and arrived at my Madison Avenue apartment in a rented Lexus, my father wearing a black suit and tie, my mother wearing a black dress with matching black heels that would somehow manage to wobble her up to the graveside. The prayers would have been said and the last rights given. Then I would have gently placed the wildflowers I had picked at the accident site and put them on the top of the casket. Then in my heart I would have gently laid her head on the casket pillow.

There would have been a gathering of friends in the Catholic church basement. My dad would have been so tall he would not have fit through any basement door. He would have looked like Mr. Bean, stooping for each doorway, followed by my mother, so tiny the top of her conservative bobbed hairdo would have been level with Julia's shoulders who would have been standing there watching, in a different state of being that I could not put my finger on.

It had become very dark. Fog had moved up from the lake to wrap itself around the double-wide like a blanket of woolly grey. I tried to find the path around to the porch but unable to see two feet in front of me, I wandered off track. I followed the edge of the gravel lane and picked my way through the murky dampness by listening to the crunch of my feet on the gravel. After walking what seemed the correct distance, I stopped. I tried to get my bearings. Deciding I had gone too far, I turned back, eyes fixed on the edge of the lane so as not to wander into the ditch. If there was a ditch. I couldn't remember.

I stopped. I knew she was close, but without visuals, my searching senses had shut down, turned off by a grey emulsion of fog thick as water.

"Where are you?" I called.

She emerged from the thin white wisps, picking her way through the grass from the roadside ditch, her sandals rustling through flowers in seven brilliant colours arranged in proper order on this August night.

"Here I am," she said.

I was hallucinating. There was no other explanation for these feelings — like waking suddenly from a dream, unable for a moment to sort out the real from the imagined — until she took my hand to guide me. Not until we reached the porch, and she stood to one side to let me come into the light did I see who she was. I picked up her hand, bent over it, studied it, my fingers stroking the naked skin. The hand was a pianist hand, each finger long and slender, each one ending in perfection, each finger filled with the capacity for the impossible.

She sat on the top step. "They're in the bedroom, both drunk, sleeping it off."

I sat beside her, shifting a little, for the step was damp.

It took time to bring myself back and ease myself forward into the explanation of peeking through the bathroom window. Finally, I told her, handed it to her, like a written confession. Her hand reached up and her fingers selected a strand of hair and drew it across her cheek. She dropped it and picked up another. She seemed uncertain, as though getting such a confession from me was not part of the plan. She planted both feet in front of her like she was feeling for secure footing. She leaned her elbows on her knees and stared at her hands. I waited, like waiting for CAT scan results.

Then she got up and went inside and after a few minutes returned with a tray and two glasses of ginger ale with ice cubes and slices of lemons. She stirred the lemon and the ice cubes in the ginger ale.

"First you take the lemon and put it on your tongue."

I hesitated.

She picked the lemon from my glass. "The rind's been cut off so you can feel the lemon on your tongue, how it melts away."

She put the lemon on my tongue. "You have to hold it and feel the sour of life and then you swallow."

I held it and then I swallowed. I watched the silvery fizzle of the ginger ale turn to bubbles and then to nothing. I watched the ice melt away and be gone.

"And now what's left, Eric, is the ginger ale, which when you drink, will take away the sour of life."

I drank.

Then she said, "I knew you were out there watching. I knew you could see and I knew what you saw. Just think how different everything would be if everyone's eyes could see souls instead of bodies."

CHAPTER TWENTY-FIVE

Eric

I woke up with a start, at first unsure of where I was. My watch said 6:00 a.m. I got up from the chesterfield. I was sure I heard someone at the front of the house.

Aiyana was not in the kitchen nor was she in the other side. I stood at the window and looked across the yard and up the lane. Hartley's Caddy was gone. For a while, I sat on the floor in the shadows of one corner on the other side. Except for the distant lap of the waves at the dock, everything was still as stone. But I felt that somewhere in the shadows, a pair of eyes was hiding, watching me, more than watching, more like observing me. I thought I heard the tinny rattle of something vibrating, a licence plate maybe. Getting up and looking out the kitchen window, I saw a car at the mailbox at the end of the lane. The mail carrier deposited letters.

When I returned to the kitchen I noticed the Red Cap lighter on the table. I peeked into Mona's bedroom. Mona was snoring, no Hartley. No Aiyana anywhere. I slipped the lighter into my pocket. I plugged in the kettle for coffee, and when the steam began to swell out of the spout, I poured the water into the filter. I sat with my cup on the porch and watched a flock of sparrows hop and peck in the grass.

I went inside and stood in the early morning sunlight, which was streaming in a long golden bar through the kitchen window and across the floor. I thought I heard a scraping against the wall of the double-wide, as though someone had accidentally brushed against the aluminum siding. I went outside and circled the double-wide and returned to the porch to listen. But the few other double-wides remaining were all completely silent. Too silent, I realized. What I was hearing now was the roar of a deathly silence.

The sun was well above the trees now, approaching seven o'clock brilliance. When I reached the sand cove, I saw halfway between the shore and Devil's Island, Uncle Jimmy's skiff drifting lazily in the sun, shining in sparkles across the flat blue. Boots on the gunwales, plaid shirt bagging over the seat, baseball hat pulled low over his eyes, cat in his lap, Hartley reclined against the side of the boat, drinking beer. Aiyana stood in the stern, right arm reaching back for her cast.

"Hey, ol' buddy!" Hartley shouted, standing, holding up the cat in one hand, the gun in the other. "We're taking the cat fishing." Throwing back his head, he drank from the bottle, leaning back so far he nearly fell overboard. Catching himself, he plunked down on the seat. He flung the empty bottle across the water and, shipping the oars, began to row toward the island. But with every third or fourth stroke, the left oar skipped across the surface so that he was gradually arcing back toward the shore. He stopped rowing and looked about, gathering his bearings. Turning the boat in the proper direction, he began again.

Shielding my eyes against the early morning sun, I waved for Aiyana to come back. She shook her head no, and waved her palm — stay away. I watched the boat zig-zag across the water toward the island. Then I dragged the canoe across the sand and climbed in and began to paddle.

Trying to get the boat heading in a straight line, Hartley did not see me coming until I was nearly broadside. By the time Hartley had dropped the oars and scrambled to his feet, I had slipped into the water. Hidden by the canoe, I could see by the shadow across the blue surface that Hartley was standing, watching for me. I kicked and dove straight down. Looking up through the wall of water overhead I saw Hartley peering down into the murky gloom below.

I crouched and kicked off, torpedoing upward and shooting out at the edge of the boat to grab Hartley who was already falling from Aiyana's grab for the cat. He fell backward into the water, arms and legs askew. The splash rained down on me and the gun arced through the air and dropped with a plunk near the shore of the island.

With one hand, I held on to the side of the boat and waited as, distorted in the shifting glass of greenish haze, Hartley kicked and thrashed two feet beneath the surface. I reached down and drew him up by the collar. But when Hartley grabbed the gunwales and tried to climb in, I pulled him away and shoved him back down. I could feel the current like two strong arms with two strong hands tugging at my ankles. I wanted to let him go with the current and would have but for Aiyana shouting, "He can't swim!"

I ferried him on his back to the other side of the island. When my feet touched the shoreline, I grasped Hartley under the arms, pulled him the rest of the way out, and sat him up on a flat rock in the sun.

Waterlogged clothes clinging in wet rags to his bony frame, Hartley sat hunched over, gasping himself into recovery. He wiped the water from his eyes and looked around. He took off his plaid shirt and pulled his t-shirt away from his skin.

I set the Red Cap lighter on the rock. "When the lighter dries out, light a fire. A forest ranger will come for you."

I followed the shoreline and swam to the boat.

...

The swim with Hartley had aggravated my shoulder. I flinched from the pain that ran from my shoulder and down my arm. Back in the double-wide, Aiyana opened the bottle of Absorbine. "Take off your shirt and sit down."

I took off my shirt and she bent to examine the purple bruise that now ran diagonally across my upper arm. She poured the green Absorbine into her palm. Her mouth set in concentration, she ran her now healed fingers back and forth across my skin. Her lips, inches from mine, were slightly parted, her eyes, usually inward, were looking directly into mine as she straightened up and poured more of the liquid into her palm. As her hand massaged from my upper arm to my shoulder, and her leg rubbed against my thigh, I could feel under this hand the swish-swish of my blood in the bruise on my shoulder and I could feel under this hand the swish-swish of her heart in the throb up my neck.

When she finished, she replaced the lid. I listened to the swish-swish of the water that was washing the hand that had rubbed my shoulder. She wiped each finger with a paper towel, one finger and then the next. Finally she said, "I'm going to tell my mother Hartley went fishing. He said he wanted to camp out on Devil's Island, roast his fresh-caught fish over the open fire, build a hut and stay overnight and cook his fish over the morning coals."

She disappeared into her mother's bedroom and told her and then went into the other side, and I was alone, listening to her footsteps that I could hear clearly crossing back and forth. With the tip of my fingers, I pushed open the door to the other side. In the light coming from one small window, I could see the outline of her body propped up in the corner of the bedroom with the ducks. I could see that she was wearing the blouse and the jeans we'd bought at the mall. But because the light was poor and the room shadowy, I could not see if she was wearing the necklace. It took all my courage to enter the room, inching forward, not sure what I wanted to see.

She sat up straight and looked up. I felt my face flush, embarrassed at being there, staring at her. She brushed one strand of hair away from her forehead. She leaned forward and drew her legs up and wrapped her arms around her knees.

"I know what my mother will do. She'll go down to the dock with a bag of Moosehead and wait for Hartley."

"So what do we do now?"

She shrugged. "Have an early lunch and then leave. But first sit with me."

I slid down beside her. We sat with our backs leaning against the wall. Across from me the ducks were watching, waiting to see what she would say next. I could hear the voice on the radio in the kitchen giving the day's Broken Deer Lake current warnings. Extreme danger. I could not remember ever hearing or even seeing a radio in the kitchen, so I got up and went in to check. I could find no radio, not in the kitchen nor in the living room. I must have imagined it. Or maybe I had put my finger on it.

Now she was leaning her back against the wall, staring at the ring of beads draped over her knee. When she shifted to give me more room, I said, "It's going to be another scorcher," opening a conversation about nothing in an attempt to get her up off the floor and ready to leave. I had to be back for work Monday and I knew I couldn't leave her here, now sitting beside me, each time she moved an arm or a leg, releasing the lingering scent of last night's bath.

Then I noticed the light from the window shining in tiny sparkles on the freshly painted red fingernails of her right hand as she reached up to take off the gold crucifix. She began to turn the cross end over end with the tips of her fingers, her eyes fixed on the circles of red in their up-and-down turning of the gold cross. She said, "When I came out of the bathroom last night, it was twelve o'clock midnight."

"But you can't tell time."

"I saw that the hands of a clock radio were both pointing straight up, two straight lines, twelve o'clock midnight."

"What clock radio?"

"Today is my birthday. Eighteen at last. If Willie were here, he'd tell you about when I was born at twelve o'clock midnight under a bright light shining from heaven, his version of being born under the big light in the OR. I was born breach. That's how come my brain got wired wrong."

She hesitated. She seemed to be struggling with what would come next. She stood and pulled me to my feet and held me. I felt her girl-woman legs against mine and I felt her warm, curving girl-woman body close to mine as she said into my ear, "Both the one you're looking for and the one you were looking at last night have been found. You're with me now, even more so than before, better than before, because now there's no space between us, because you've seen me naked."

CHAPTER TWENTY-SIX

Aiyana

We packed our stuff into the Wrangler and headed off. Passing through the Broken Deer Double-Wides gate, I watched one lone gull swing away from the others, riding the wind in a wide arc, disappearing for a moment and then returning with a second gull, like one white feather, riding the thermals and finding its mate. I shut my eyes and leaned back against the head rest. Sunlight slanted upon me, washing over me, suspending me in drowsy contentment.

The soothing music playing on the Kicker, the soft leather of the Wrangler seats made me feel safe, like inside the church's picket fence. Socks nestled in my lap, the little motor running, must have felt the same. I settled back and relaxed.

When I woke up, we were turning off the 401. I straightened up and shifted in the seat. I said, "I used to watch that program Find the Music when I was about seven, me sitting on one end of the couch, my mother passed out on the other, and on the satellite flatscreen, the little pianists in frilly frocks with the mommies and the daddies and the aunties in gowns and tuxedos. It's a program for little kids in glass slippers who all think they're going to Juilliard. Forget Juilliard. I'm eighteen now. I'm an adult now. I'm not sitting on my couch watching Find the Music and dreaming of being the concert pianist. Now I'm sitting in this Wrangler deciding to get a job."

...

Although I was familiar with Eric's Madison Avenue apartment, compared to the double-wide, it seemed like a fancy penthouse. It was like I'd never seen such luxury, except on TV: wall-to-wall carpeting, expensive furniture, brass floor lamps, an open-concept kitchen with a chrome stove and refrigerator gleaming in the overhead lights. A glance along the hallway showed a bathroom tiled floor to ceiling. I couldn't believe I'd never noticed any of this before. It was like I'd left this apartment wearing mismatched socks and worn-out slippers and retuned wearing a gown and glass slippers. It's like I'd left as a teenager and returned as an adult.

Eric sat opposite me. He crossed one leg over the other. "You mentioned you cleaned the church. That's custodial. Let me have a look." He opened his laptop. "Econo Maid, Molly Maid, Janitorial Services — wait, Meat Wrapper? What's that doing there? — Here's one. Custodial. Roy Thomson Hall."

I had watched concerts at Roy Thomson on TV. I flexed my fingers gently. "Yeah. That would be a nice place to work."

Later, at the Roy Thomson Hall interview, Eric sat next to me, saying nothing as the head custodian asked a few polite questions. Then came the problem.

"How far did you go in school?"

Eric said, "She didn't go far, but up north there aren't many schools. And she travelled around a lot with her grandfather. Her reading skills are poor, but she's not afraid of work."

The man looked doubtful. "The problem is, we use hazardous chemicals. You have to be able to read the labels to know which to use where. If you mix the wrong two chemicals … poof." He threw up his hands.

"How about just sweeping?" suggested Eric. "Picking up trash, taking out the garbage."

He agreed to give me a try on the night shift, eleven o'clock until two, five nights a week. Eric didn't like the idea of me being downtown at two in the morning. But the head custodian assured him that two in the morning downtown was no different than two in the afternoon. "Like New York, Toronto never sleeps. Besides, she'll be working with Isabella and Maria, and they take the subway."

...

I arrived at the back entrance of Roy Thomson a few minutes before eleven. Neither Maria nor Isabella spoke much English. They showed me where the brooms and dustpans and garbage cart were kept. They set me to work in the balcony, brushing off the seats and sweeping the aisles, top row first, working my way down. A second crew with mops and vacuums did the tile floors and the carpets.

I expected a stage filled with instruments: strings, woodwinds, brass, percussion, and most of all, the piano. But by eleven at night, the stage was bare and everyone had gone home and only the pictures in the front lobby suggested what musicians had been there before I arrived.

Give thanks to the Angel of Mercy, I told myself, as every evening I swept floors and picked up garbage. I was earning my own money, my fingers had healed, my foot was better, and most of all, I was safe. No more Hartley hammering on Eric's door now fitted with two deadbolts and two chain locks with bolt-cutter guards.

But, of course, I did wonder how my mother was doing. It wasn't like me asking myself, I wonder how she's doing. The wondering was more like a memory of a woman I had once known but needed to leave behind so I could get on with my life. But she was giving me wide-awake dreams that broke me out in shivers. She wore rubber boots. She kept goldfish in a rain barrel, about ten of them all swimming around at the bottom. Since they all looked the same, she called them all Hartley. She'd put on her rubber boots. 'I'm going to feed Hartley,' she'd say, as though there was only one. When winter came the water in the barrel froze solid and that was the end of Hartley.

CHAPTER TWENTY-SEVEN

Eric

Spring arrived and April came and, as though Aiyana and I were back in almost the exact spot we started, I decided to make the pork chops, not with mushroom soup but with asparagus soup. And this time not cooked to boot leather. Aiyana dressed for dinner, looking wholesome and healthy in her new white blouse and designer blue jeans. She looked older and more mature, elegant in fact, and rested, the fatigue lines gone from under her eyes. When she ran her hand through her hair, every time she did that, I noticed — stronger than noticed, marvelled — that her fingernails were clean and glossy.

She was relaxed and happy. "Finally, I'm beginning to like it here. Everyone looks different than everyone else: Black, white, brown, turbans, those little beanies without the propellers, that's Jewish. Like mismatched socks, which means everyone looks the same, because we're all socks."

I served the dinner; Aiyana sat opposite me at the table. "Last night at work I learned about Beethoven: Did deafness drive him to create his masterpieces or did deafness prevent him from creating greater masterpieces?"

That was why, that was the trigger, while driving her to the subway along Huron Street, when I noticed a sign in the front window of a house — Two Bed for Rent — I said, "Let's check it out."

I pulled over to the curb and we got out of the car and stood looking up at the arched windows along the second floor and the single attic window under the eaves.

"This looks nice," I said. "Sort of rustic." I started up the walk, Aiyana following. We climbed the steps of the front porch and rang the bell. A young woman with short hair wearing a sweatshirt and jeans opened the door. She introduced herself as Charlene. She led the way up a carpeted stairway to the second floor. "My parents are the landlords. They live next door. But I look after everything."

At the top of the stairs to the right, a door opened into a large dining room, a small but new kitchen, two bedrooms, and a large bath.

Charlene said, "Two thousand a month, and we'll need first and last."

Aiyana said, "Yeah, I think so. I think this will be all right."

Charlene said, "New fridge." She pointed at it. "New stove. It's electric. You don't have to worry about that." She opened the cupboards and looked inside. "Just checking. Never know what you might find." She opened the cutlery drawer. "Spoons and knives and stuff go in here. We buy our cutlery at Goodwill. Last week my dad bought a complete carving set because it was half price. He said, 'Thanksgiving is coming.' I said, 'Duh. It's April.' I said, 'Duh. There's only two of us. A turkey is twenty pounds.'"

Eric said, "We have a cat."

"A cat, yeah. Okay."

"And a piano."

Aiyana gave me a startled look, which I ignored.

Charlene hesitated. "Hmm. A piano. Okay. But no music after eleven. But first you have to fill out an application. We check employment and references."

I gave her my business card. "Tell your dad I'm an accountant with the IRS."

She wasn't impressed. "First and last by the end of the day. But first the app."

Then we heard a rasping sound coming from somewhere nearby. Aiyana seemed shaken, frightened in fact. "What's that noise?"

"One of the tenants in the bachelor next door, an old man. He's sleeping. That's how he snores."

I listened to the wheeze of the old man's lungs sawing their way through his sleep.

"I'll leave it to you guys to figure it out." Charlene disappeared down the stairs.

While I stood by the doorway, my shoulder leaning against the frame, Aiyana checked the closets, the cupboard, the bathroom, like ticking off a list. The last thing to check was the walk-in closet in the bedroom.

Aiyana stood by the closet door, listening. The guttural wheeze of the man's snoring seemed to grow louder, seeping through the closet walls from the other side. "It sounds like the ice moving on the shoreline. In the spring it would do that. In April."

"Ice?"

"Trapped in the rocks, rasping around with the waves boiling it up and down…"

I knew what was coming, so I waited.

"Hartley is down there. I know it. He'll surface when the ice comes out."

I stood by the door, my right hand resting on the cold doorknob. "I left him on the shore. He was fine."

Blinking away the tears, she stared at me. "I think we shouldn't live here. We'll find another apartment." She wiped at her eyes. "I can't live here."

We went down the stairs and into the street. I watched her disappear down the subway steps on her way to the tunnel that would take her to Roy Thomson.

CHAPTER TWENTY-EIGHT

Eric

I had stopped off after work to buy groceries, so I was an hour late coming home. Aiyana was sitting on the front step. She'd forgotten her keys. She stood beside me and waited for me to unlock the outer door. I began to put away the groceries. She sat at the kitchen table and stared at a spot on the floor directly in front of her sandalled feet. She tucked them under her chair and studied her hands that lay palms up in her lap. She brought one hand up to worry one strand of hair. Next the playing with the crucifix. Then the long silence as the electric current from the other side plugged itself into her special edition intuition on this side and Thinking began to think her.

That's what it looked like.

Finished with the groceries, I sat with her at the table to wait for these thoughts to get formed into words. She'd gone blank. Her eyes, velvety black and distant, revealed no hint of emotion. Apart from her frowning, contemplatively chewing the inside of her cheek, she seemed absent. When the hand that had been curling and uncurling the strand of hair strayed to her mouth, I put my hand on hers before she could start on her fingernails.

Then she began. "Last night was Cinderella. I was remembering Father Clark would say we only see the world once and that is in childhood. The rest is simply replaying what happened to us as a child. I think the world you saw in childhood was a nice house with garbage collection three times a week and swing sets in the playground and tea sets with little cups to drink from. Well, not teacups. Whatever little boys play with in Florida or Boston or wherever it was. For bedtime tuck-in your mother probably came into your bedroom with your own little TV to watch Little Mary Sunshine or, well probably, Sesame Street, and all your toys lined up on a shelf and nice shirts and sweaters in nice drawers to give you a nice kiss.

"My mother was always so drunk and so fat I'd have to be careful she didn't sit on me for tuck-in, if there was one. I'd hide my head in the pillow so she wouldn't slobber her beer spit on me for a goodnight kiss, if there was one. Where I come from there are no playgrounds with swing sets to play on and no tea sets to drink from. The kids play Pass Out. They stumble around and fall down in the dirt, imitating uncle somebody or aunt somebody. So by the end of last night I wasn't thinking Cinderella. All I was thinking was the garbage left behind for me to pick up after Cinderella was over.

"So I looked up and I looked around and I saw what you would see: rows of nice seats sitting on expensive carpeting and nice rich people in suits and gowns with nice cars parked outside. So I looked up and I looked around and I saw what I saw: the derelict cars and derelict people and the derelict dogs and derelict double-wides.

"So then I noticed one of the custodial guys was giving me a bush-bait look, standing right there looking at me the way Hartley did. So I asked him to dial my mother's number on his cellphone and ask how Hartley's doing. I watched him listen on his phone and hang up. He said they found Hartley yesterday, washed up on shore when the ice came out."

I wanted to shut this door before she got it open. "No, Aiyana. No way. I left him with your Red Cap lighter, alive and kicking on the other side of Devil's Island. I told him when the lighter dries out, light a fire. The forest ranger will come."

Her searchlight eyes fastened on mine. She said, "You left him with my Red Cap lighter? I can't believe it."

"All he had to do, Aiyana, was light a fire with that lighter that you said would burn eternally."

Her eyes filled with tears and her lips began to tremble. "Eric, I told you. Hartley couldn't light that lighter. The only one who can light that lighter is my dad and the only one he will light it for is me."

She thought for a moment. "I'm sorry. Without an Understanding Aiyana guidebook, how would you know that?"

She wiped at her tears in one direction, trying to take them away, and then in the other direction trying to put them back. "There's a reason why people like me fall in love with people like you. You stand with both feet on this side."

I stood and pulled her to her feet and held her. But she broke away. "I'm sorry. I'm wanted at Roy Thomson. Time to go."

"It's too early. Your shift doesn't start until eleven."

"I think they need me early."

"Why do you think that? Did they phone?"

"I just know, I just know, like choosing Grandpa Willie, I just knew."

CHAPTER TWENTY-NINE

Aiyana

When I opened the rear door of Roy Thomson Hall, I was surprised to hear the symphony tuning up. The head custodian explained, "You're here early, Aiyana. They haven't finished their practice. You have to wait for the musicians to leave the stage before you start to work."

I climbed to the balcony with my broom and dustpan. The musicians were waiting for the conductor, who arrived from backstage. He was tall and thin. He looked creepy with his black shirt open to the waist of his leather pants. He stood before them and began to talk in an accent that I knew was German from watching war movies.

"Beethoven's Fifth. The first movement is urgent and grim with short moments of sadness. Then the coda is restless until it seems to get tired, and then a few final chords end the first movement."

I glanced from one musician to the next.

"In the second movement, the theme is elegant and bolder, more triumphant, and also a little tentative in parts. Then the third movement starts darkly, but after a while the first theme comes back, reminding us of the earlier movements, but a little sunnier. Then the mood gets murky, and you can sense something is coming. Then the fourth movement, so joyful it can't contain itself as it triumphs over the first and the second. From this point on is heart-pumping celebration and jubilation."

I had no idea what he was talking about, nor had I ever heard Beethoven's Fifth, that I knew of. Then the orchestra began, but not for long. The conductor waved his baton for a halt. They began again and again and again until they managed to get it right. Finally, the musicians left the stage, taking their instruments with them, leaving only the Hamburg Steinway.

I was the only trailer-park kid at the Sudbury Music Festival. The other girls wore nice white dresses and nice white knee socks and sparkling black shoes. But I had to wear the same old dress. My mother was supposed to take me but had a hangover. So Grandpa Willie said he'd drive me. I started to cry because I couldn't find two matching socks. He didn't go and find the socks for me and make me feel stupider than I already felt. He said, "You don't need two matching socks." But I knew I did because I knew I should look like little Miss Find the Music, not like some trailer-park weirdo with mismatched socks.

I sat in the front row with all the other little girls who were playing. The stage was huge, like it was floating ten feet high, and the piano was huge, and the steps leading up to the stage were huge, and when I got up there and looked around the auditorium at all the people, about three hundred huge people, they were all looking at me. I started to cry because standing in the spotlight way up in the air like that, everyone could see my socks.

Willie got up from the back row. When he came down the aisle and up onto the stage, I saw how huge he was, bigger than all the people, bigger than the stage and bigger than the piano. He knelt beside me and he whispered, "Don't worry about your socks. These people are not here to look at your socks; they're here to hear you play."

So then he took my hand and helped me onto the piano stool and I started to play, not for the three hundred people, but for my Grandpa Willie, and all of a sudden I didn't feel like a scruffy trailer-park weirdo who couldn't tell colours and couldn't match socks. I felt like Cinderella dancing in my glass slippers to my own music with my prince.

CHAPTER THIRTY

I, Anna

Wolfram Sagaarman gave each piece his own unique interpretation. He was proud of his relentless perfectionism. It was in his blood, he never tired of saying, and never tired of reminding anyone who played for him. Beethoven's Fifth in C Minor was rich enough that the possibilities were endless, but not easily achieved.

Sagaarman was seated backstage, reviewing the notes he'd made on the practice session he'd just finished and occasionally giving glances to the cellist, an attractive young man. But the cellist was not glancing back. He was peeking at something through the curtains. Sagaarman listened carefully for a moment. He got up to look at the stage.

Dressed in a blue cleaning smock, her hair pulled back in a ponytail, her broom lying on the floor beside her, her dustpan propped against one leg of the piano stool, a girl sat at the Hamburg Steinway. She was already well into the first movement of the piece he'd just finished practising. Sagaarman tiptoed to a seat in the front row. By the time the cleaning girl had finished her interpretation of Beethoven's Fifth all the members of the New York Philharmonic had followed him to the front row.

Sagaarman knew that many pianists had the hands but not the ear, and some had the hands and the ear but not the absolute pitch; very few had the hands, the ear, and absolute pitch as well as synchronicity, the supernatural ability to get behind the score and into the composer's psyche and follow the composer's inner pulse.

He came up onto the stage and sat beside her on the piano bench. "What's your name?"

"Aiyana. I'm sorry. I should have asked permission."

"And you work here as a cleaner. What school of music are you attending?"

"I never went to school."

"You must have gone to school. A gifted program. Which one?"

"I taught myself."

"Where are you from?"

"Broken Deer Double-Wides. Near Sudbury."

"Is that a place?"

"Sort of."

"Where have you played, professionally I mean?"

"Nowhere."

"How do you know this Beethoven?"

"I heard you practising it."

"But you've never played it before."

"I don't know. I don't know their names. I just play them."

"Ah." Sagaarman nodded. "What else could you play for me tonight?"

"I like Chopin."

"Which one?"

"I don't know. It's hard to keep them separate. I just play what comes to me."

"Because you've heard them somewhere."

"They just come to me."

"Ah," said Sagaarman, nodding. "Have you ever heard of acausal parallelism? We call it wrong time. Right notes. In music, it's when two people unrelated in time and place are able to create identical note- and chord-sequencing, like the one through intuition is tuned into the other. Do you know what I mean?"

"When I was little I thought I was two people."

"Ah, yes. I have only once met someone like you and that is how she described it. You have the rarest of gifts. With your permission, I'd like to put together a late-night panel — it's nine o'clock in the evening, but they'll come and listen if I tell them."

"Can they get me into Juilliard?"

"If that is where you want to go, then yes. I'm sure that can be arranged."

. . .

By ten o'clock two men and one woman had arrived. Still in her cleaning uniform, the girl seated herself at the piano.

"We'll sit in the front row," Sagaarman said. "Pretend we're not here."

He watched her stretch each finger, bending each one back before playing the scales, her right hand first up and down, and then her left, sizing up the piano's character and idiosyncrasies, her natural talent matching itself to the instrument. She leaned forward, curling herself around the keyboard, settling in. And then she started, or rather the music started, or maybe neither started. Maybe it wasn't about starting but about the one becoming the other, and she was gone, like somewhere a switch had tripped, flooding the stage with her presence as concert became séance, first from Rondo in C Minor and then seamlessly into Polonaise in E flat, then seamlessly into Revolutionary Etude until, when she launched into the impossible demands of Chopin's Fantasia, Sagaarman climbed onto the stage and put his hand on her shoulder to stop her, for by this time she had beaten her fingers raw and her nails were bleeding.

END